Praise for

FIRE
FROM THE
SKY

Printz Award Honor

Cooperative Children's Book Center Best of the Year

Kirkus Best of the Year

✶ "*Fire from the Sky* is a superb account of one boy's struggle to be himself. Åstot does an exemplary job invoking Sami culture, and an especially good job of capturing Ante's turbulent emotions, dramatically ratcheting up tension, as it is often agony for Ante to be around the friend he's so in love with. Much of Ante's experience is universal, and empathic readers will hope urgently for his happiness." —*Booklist* (starred)

✶ "A rare and triumphant look at what it means for queerness to stay put, with all the messiness and pain that entails… A fresh voice and a setting that's pure fire." —*Kirkus* (starred)

FIRE FROM THE SKY

Moa Backe Åstot

Translated by EVA APELQVIST

FIRE FROM THE SKY

Lantern
Paperbacks

This is a Lantern Paperback
Published by Levine Querido

www.levinequerido.com • info@levinequerido.com

Levine Querido is distributed by Chronicle Books, LLC
Read more about Moa Backe Åstot at
rabensjogren.se

Originally published in Sweden in 2021 by Rabén & Sjögren

ISBN: 978-1-64614-556-0
Printed and bound in China

MIX
Paper | Supporting responsible forestry
FSC™ C144853
FSC
www.fsc.org

First Lantern Paperback Edition: April 2025
First Printing

For Áhkko.
Ähtsáv duv.

ÁNTE STARED AT the blinking cursor in the search bar until his pulse began beating in sync with it. He tried to resist, but something tugged at him. His fingers hesitated when he wrote. He closed his eyes for a second before he looked at the search results. Several threads had appeared on the forum Flashback. He read the caption of the topmost one.

Before he could read the actual post, his thumb found the Lock-Screen button on his phone. The screen immediately turned black, erasing the words that had pulled him in. But they were still there. They filled his entire being.

Do homosexual reindeer herders exist?

ÁNTE'S FINGERS CLOSED around the reindeer's antlers. The strong bull reacted immediately. It yanked at his arm, refused to give in. Just then Ánte caught sight of Erik on the other side of the corral. Brown-bear eyes trained at him.

Their gaze froze when they looked at each other.

Ánte's body softened; he lost his grip of the reindeer and fell. The snow had been trampled into the consistency of flour; his feet and knees sank deep, stuck. The sound of reindeer mixed with the shouts from the other herders. The reindeer surrounded him, moving round and round. He closed his eyes. But despite everything, he felt safe here, right where he fell—he knew that the reindeer would not trample him as long as there was another way.

His body could still feel Erik's gaze. Burning through layer after layer of heavy winter clothing.

He was still scrambling to get up on to his feet when he heard Erik's melodious calling in the dark. A reindeer was trying to pull away from Erik, but without success. From a distance it looked like they were playing.

The snow was coming down fast, painting white dots in the black sky. It was almost night and the members of the Sámi village had worked all day separating the reindeer in the herd. Ánte's pulse quickened as he hurried up to Erik. Together they dragged the bull into Ánte's family pen—the enclosure where his family's reindeer were gathered. When they turned to head back to the corral, Ánte almost stumbled into Erik. He had no control over his own body. It didn't work like it should and every muscle hurt.

"Are you tired?" Erik asked. "We can probably take a break soon."

Ánte shook his head, took off his glove and wiped his eye. Erik's smile blurred around the edges.

His hand on Ánte's shoulder.

"Soon, buddy."

THEY WERE SITTING ON TWO tree stumps, encircling the fire with their snowy boots. Erik was drinking scalding-hot boiled coffee from his gukse; Ánte was counting seconds, stopped at thirty-two, which is when Julia arrived. She sat down close to Erik, buried her red nose in his neck. Put her hand inside his coat.

"Let's head home soon, okay?"

Erik shook his head.

"There's still reindeer in the run. We'll have a few more corrals worth."

He looked at Ánte, who nodded. Julia's knit cap was covered in white. Her whole body was shaking.

"Use my extra coat. It's in the bag."

Erik's own coat was unzipped down his chest, and his hat was in his lap while they rested. His bangs were glued to his sweaty forehead. Ánte wanted to lean over and brush them aside. Move Erik's hair behind his ear, move his fingers down Erik's neck.

He kept his hand perfectly still in his glove.

Erik kissed Julia just under the edge of her hat before he stood up and shook the fresh snow from his snow pants. Ánte should have stood up too, should have done a lot of things that he never did, but his body felt numb.

"Are you coming?"

Erik stood by the gate to the pen. The corral was about to fill up again—you could hear the reindeer coming. He lifted an eyebrow. When Ánte gave no response whatsoever, he left.

The reindeer came thundering in. The sound of bells and hooves on the snow filled Ánte's chest with an enormous longing. Or missing. He couldn't identify the feeling, didn't know where it came from. Because he was right here. There was nothing to miss.

Julia looked at him from across the fire. It looked like she was about to say something.

"What?"

She didn't answer, just shrugged and turned away from him. Ánte stayed for a moment before he forced himself up on his feet. He walked over to the reindeer, slamming the gate behind him. It didn't shut all the way; he had to do it again, more carefully, before it closed.

He went into the middle of the herd. People and reindeer pushed past him, shoving him with their arms, backs, antlers. He tried to look for earmarks that he recognized among hundreds of ears, but he couldn't focus.

He startled when somebody shoved him.

"What are you doing, standing around like a bum?"

Ánte turned to his dad. For a moment they looked at each other quietly. Then his dad caught a reindeer practically without looking and Ánte grabbed the other antler. The first instinct was always to help.

They pulled. Ánte didn't know if he was any help at all, if there was even any strength left in his arm. Maybe his father's strength was the only thing moving the reindeer forward.

Ánte's grandmother was standing on a tree stump in order to see over the fence into the corral. She checked the reindeer off as it was let into the pen.

With a shaky hand she wrote down the name of the reindeer's owner.

"Find one for yourself now," she said, patting Ánte on his back, between his shoulder blades.

"Yes, Áhkko."

"Are you cold?"

He shook his head.

"Sweating."

Áhkko was wearing her large down coat. Her wild-strawberry-colored hat made her head look round, like a little berry.

"Maybe you need a little break."

Ánte's dad had gone back to the pasture. He had already grabbed another large bull and started dragging it toward the pen. The reindeer was swinging its antlers, throwing its head toward Ánte's father's face.

Ánte took a deep breath; his lungs filled with air. Behind his rib cage, his heart had not calmed down. It beat as if there was nothing else in the world to beat for but this.

"Maybe later," he said.

THE SNOW-COVERED STREETS of Jokkmokk were crowded. It was market Saturday and people from all over the world were making their way among the booths. Some wore gábde, colorful fabrics that caught the eye. Others were dressed in big furs and fox hats, or snow pants and snowmobile boots. Like Ánte. He was dressed in all gray. His cousin Ida, walking next to him, had pulled her blue njálmmefáhta on over her coat. Ánte felt like a tourist—he regretted his choice of clothing.

He looked over at the friend that Ida had brought, Hanna. They all went to the same school, but Ánte couldn't remember having ever spoken to her. She smiled when she noticed him watching her. Her cheeks were red from the cold.

By one of the booths a Sámi flag moved in the wind. Two tourists, a man and a woman, had stopped beneath it to take pictures of each other. Ánte looked at the colors. Red for fire, green for all growing things. Blue for water and yellow for the sun. The woman was beaming under the flag.

Hanna's voice made him turn around.

"Why aren't you wearing your gábdde? They're so nice."

"Didn't feel like it," he said.

Hanna knit her eyebrows; maybe she couldn't hear him. Or maybe she just didn't understand what he meant.

"It would be super cool to have one," she said. "Do you get one if you marry a Sámi?"

He shrugged, but his gesture was barely noticeable in the crowd.

Ida stopped to buy a raspberry donut. The smell mixed with the smell of suovas, smoked reindeer meat, and polkagris, peppermint candy. Music was playing in the distance but where Ánte, Ida and Hanna stood, the only thing you could hear was the bass. The ground vibrated slightly under their feet. All around them, people floated by. A Mylar balloon in the shape of a lime green dinosaur had been tied to the handle of a stroller. The dinosaur's mouth was open to the sky, trying to swallow the tiny snowflakes.

Ánte shoved Ida.

"You want a balloon like that? Maybe there's a pink one?"

"Ánte," Ida said. "Hanna and I were nice to let you come along so maybe you should try to not be a geek."

He shook his head and picked out a rainbow-colored marmalade cube from the plastic bag he was carrying, the sugar sticky on his fingertips. He put the candy in his mouth and wiped his hand on the rustling surface of his snow pants. His fingers turned stiff from the cold before he could get his glove back on.

Then he noticed Hanna's look. Warm and soft. As if she was trying not to laugh.

"You're funny," she said.

"Thank you?"

"A bit over the top," Ida added. "But look who's coming!"

Ánte saw him right away through the crowd, the blue fabric of the gábdde, the bright red details. Across Erik's chest, his shiny blue sliehppá, the collar embellished with pewter thread designs. He had a belt tied around his waist, and on his arm, a girl. Julia was wearing a black coat and black snow pants, a shadow next to him. She clung tightly to his arm as they pushed their way through the crowd. It looked like she was afraid to lose him.

Ida's mouth was wide open; you could see the donut inside. Some raspberry jam had gotten stuck in the corner of her mouth. Hanna shook her head at Ida's reaction.

"Oh god, he's actually insanely good-looking."

Ánte stared at Ida as if she had lost her mind.

"Who? God?"

She rolled her eyes under frozen eyelashes.

Ánte was quiet, wishing Ida would be too, but they didn't seem to have any genetic material in common whatsoever. She waved frantically in Erik and Julia's direction, but they didn't see her. They soon disappeared into the crowd.

A large man pushed his way past the three of them and Hanna's back was shoved into Ánte's chest. She giggled. How could she be so cheerful? Now? There was barely room to breathe. He would never go to the market on a Saturday again. Why would you expose yourself to something like this?

Hanna stood so close to Ánte now that he could almost feel her lips on his ear.

"Honestly," she said, "I don't really think he's that good-looking."

"Who? God?"

"Stop it!" she shouted, right into his ear canal. He made a face from the deafening sound.

Somebody else came so close to them that Ánte and Hanna were pushed into each other again. Ida was nowhere to be found. Where did she go? Ánte's heart was beating so hard it hurt.

There was not enough air. He knew for sure—they were about to run out. Very soon there would be no more air and besides, Hanna was standing much too close and she was talking too much and he could no longer hear what she was saying.

He gathered courage, raised his voice.

"Heading over to the Sámi Educational Center," he said. "They're selling books there."

He couldn't hear Hanna's answer; she seemed to be looking for Ida. He escaped. Fought his way out of the market area as quickly as possible.

He didn't care if the others were behind him.

THE HEAT INSIDE the school thawed his cheeks. A door to the left led to the room that served as a used bookstore during market days. Inside, books were spread out across tables and lined up on shelves along the walls.

Soon he heard the girls by the front door. Ida and Hanna were laughing loudly at something. It cut through the room. Ánte kept moving until he reached a shelf at the very far corner of the room, tried to get his breath to slow down.

A voice startled him.

"Find anything?"

When Ánte turned around, he was right there. Erik.

For a moment they stood so close that Ánte could have touched him if he only reached out a little. He allowed his eyes to follow the pewter thread embroidery on Erik's sliehppá, and up toward his face. A birthmark in the tiny indentation under his nose. Another on his cheek. A third one just under his eyelashes. Three tiny brown dots. Like a constellation.

Erik's eyes made his body tremble. He was frozen.

He didn't blink for several seconds, hours, years.

"Hellooo? Are you buying something?"

He tried to focus on the books. Tried to read the covers, but he didn't understand what he was reading. The letters just floated around, wouldn't line up. His brain refused to cooperate.

"Maybe." He grabbed a book without looking. "This one. You?"

Erik shook his head.

"Ida dragged us over here. Hanna said you were here."

Ánte glanced toward Ida and Hanna, who were still standing by the door. Julia had joined them. Hanna was pointing at a book. Whatever she saw on the cover caused her to put her hands in front of her mouth.

"Hey, you, over there," Ida called amid bouts of laughter. "Are we leaving, or what?"

It had turned dark outside, but the market booths lit their way as they walked. Snowflakes danced in the dark, landed in Erik's hair like sprinkles. Ánte glanced at him now and then. Tried to remember a time when he had not felt like this. A time before everything had become about Erik. He could barely imagine it. He could not think of Erik any other way, even though he knew it had not always felt like this. It had begun slowly, a close friendship, a feeling of wanting to be even closer. A feeling of suffocating when he was too far away.

The girls were still having fun with something that Ánte didn't understand. He was freezing. His skin was getting damp. He didn't have a bag for the book and he tried to protect it with his leather gloves. Erik nodded at it and asked if he could look. A wrinkle appeared between his eyebrows when he read the back. Then he tore off the price tag. Held it on his fingertip for a moment, stuck it on Ánte's coat sleeve.

"A hundred nineteen kronor for you today."

Ánte took the book back. "Would you have bought me?"

Erik laughed and shook his head. "I only have a one-hundred-kronor bill left."

ÁNTE THREW THE BOOK on his bed. His duvet cover got damp. He lay down next to the book and held it up in front of his face. He didn't even know what he had bought—his escape attempt had cost him 119 kronor.

The light from his bedside lamp reached the cover of the book. *Racial Types in North Bothnia.*

Beneath the title was a tiny, sketched portrait. A gray face. The man looked worn, old, wrinkled.

The smell of paper was strong when he opened the book and began flipping through it. A soothing smell over disturbing words. Black-and-white photos were spread across some of the pages. Sámis, mountains and goade. A photograph of three people: a woman with long braids, a man wearing a coat and a hat—almost twice as tall as the man in gábdde next him. The hat man's eyes were dark behind his glasses.

Harald Lundgren with the North Bothnic Sámi Anta, and Anta's wife, Sigga.

Ánte stared at the shorter man. His face wore a dogged expression. Dark, as if he was standing in the shade. *Anta.* Almost like Ánte. His thumb moved gently over the picture.

A few pages later he found more photos. Several heads, photographed from different angles. The caption said *Laplander types.* Empty, cold stares, dark holes instead of eyes. It was obvious that they had not agreed to being photographed. He shivered. A dark feeling seeped into his backbone and settled there.

Photographer: H Lundgren, Uppsala. Ánte froze, lowered his arm. Lundgren—that man again.

After the portraits came a few pictures of naked bodies; from the front, from the back, in profile. Men, women. Even children. He paused at one of the photos, almost ashamed to look. A child stood stiffly and uncomfortably, arms hanging down its sides. Eyes full of fear.

The book landed on the mattress. He turned off the light next to his bed and the room turned dark. Not black, but gray. Gray, gray, gray.

He felt something in his gut. Something had awoken suddenly, something that tried crawling up his throat. He swallowed and swallowed, but the feeling kept forcing its way up.

Then he just lay there, staring into the dark. In the shadows, nothing had colors.

A KNOCK ON the front door made Ánte drop his phone on the table. Who would visit at this hour? Late evening. He'd only just gotten up on his feet when Erik stood in the doorway between the entryway and the kitchen, snow melting into droplets around his boots. When he took off his snowmobile hat, his hair stood out every which way. It was a hurricane. He ran his fingers through his hair.

What was he doing here? Didn't they lock the front door? Even though they were close friends, Erik had never come over this late. Ánte's heart tried beating its way out of his rib cage.

"Are you awake?" Erik asked.

"No," Ánte said, lifting a teacup to his mouth. Tried to keep his voice steady. "I'm asleep, sitting up."

It might be true. He felt like he was dreaming.

"I thought I saw a light through the window." Erik scratched his head. "But maybe it was somebody else."

"That's weird. Everybody here's asleep," Ánte said. "If you listen carefully, you can hear me snore."

Erik's smile made Ánte swallow too hard. His throat burned.

"What are you even doing up this late?"

"Couldn't sleep." Erik removed his bag from his back, leaned it against his leg. "I brought a snack. Maybe we could head out."

Head out? In the middle of the night?

"How did you know I was awake?"

"You have a pelt we can bring, right?" Erik asked, heading out into the hallway.

Ánte stood up and poured his tea into the sink. It smelled of hay and vanilla. The cup clinked against the sink when he put it down.

"You keep them in the garage?"

Erik had already stepped back into his shoes and pulled his cap on when Ánte came out into the entryway. Ánte put his snow pants on and shoved his feet into his boots. Erik took a key from the wooden key cabinet on the wall and went outside.

Ánte hurried out behind him. There was a light on in the garage—the smell of gasoline and snowmobile reached them before they entered. Inside, Erik took a tightly rolled reindeer pelt from the floor, then turned off the light before he came back outside and handed the key to Ánte. The metal had turned warm in Erik's hand. Ánte pressed it against the palm of his own hand.

THE WOODS WERE QUIET around them; everything was quiet. The only sounds were twigs snapping under their feet and their own breaths in the crisp air. They walked slowly, as if not to wake what was asleep. When they arrived at the frozen lake, Erik tapped down the snow, spread the reindeer pelt on the ground and sat down. Ánte sat down next to him.

"Times like these you're happy you don't live in Jokkmokk," Erik said. "I don't think it's ever quiet there on market nights."

Ánte leaned back on the pelt and watched the stars.

The sky was endless above them. Tiny twinkling spots in the vast darkness. A net of pearls.

He felt small where he lay. Smaller than a dot. High above them figures were floating around. He thought about the Sámi constellations that Áhkko had told him about. Not many people saw them anymore, but she did. He looked at the North Star that held up the sky. And the gigantic moose, Sarvva, that the hunters pursued, caught in an eternal chase. If the hunter Fávdna caught up with the moose and shot his arrow toward it, it was said, he might mistakenly hit the North Star, where the sky was attached. Then the sky would fall down and crush the earth. The world would catch on fire. Go down, once and for all.

He wondered if the hunter would dare to shoot when the whole world was at stake. Was it worth it, risking that much? To win, or to lose everything.

But maybe this was when it would happen. Maybe the time was now.

"What are you looking at?"

Ánte, startled, turned to look at Erik.

"Just the constellations."

"Aha."

Erik lay down too. His head ended up very close to Ánte's. They stayed like that, quiet. Ánte focused on counting the stars. Pretended that his face wouldn't touch Erik's if he turned over on his side. Pretended that his body was not running out of oxygen.

"Feel like a snack?" Erik said. "There's fruit in the bag."

"Okay."

Erik sat up and pulled the leather bag closer. He took out a yellow orange. His fingertips shone when he peeled it, white fragments caught under his nails. When he had stripped away the outer layer, he broke the fruit open. The inside glowed red, like blood.

He sucked on a section, handed one to Ánte, who took off his gloves. The juice stuck to the corner of his mouth.

"Do you think our ancestors also sat here eating blood oranges by the lake in the winter?" Erik asked.

Ánte snorted, put his hand in front of his mouth to prevent the piece of orange from falling out. He shook his head, swallowed hard.

"I don't think they had blood oranges back then."

When Erik grinned widely, tiny creases formed around his eyes. Ánte wanted to touch them but instead he put his wet fingers against one other. They had gotten a little wrinkled.

"That book you bought," Erik said. "What was it about? Really?"

The black-and-white photographs were still vivid in Ánte's mind.

The bodies, the frightened look on the child's face. He had thought about them all evening, had tossed and turned until he had finally given up trying to fall asleep.

"Don't know. Old stuff."

"Is that why you're suddenly an expert on ancestors and blood oranges?"

Ánte pulled his knees to his body and shook his head. Put his hands against his cheeks.

"Are you cold?" Erik asked.

"No. A little."

Erik moved closer, wiped the palms of his hands on his thighs. Then he reached for Ánte's face with one hand.

The entire firmament moved into Ánte's body.

"I'm warm," Erik said. "Feel this."

He put the palm of his hand on Ánte's left cheek. It burned. His thumb moved softly over Ánte's skin, made the other cheek scream to be touched. Ánte tried to control his breath, focused on the birthmark above Erik's lip. The tiny brown dot.

What was happening? Ánte was cold and Erik warm, he really was—maybe he just wanted to help warm Ánte? But there was still a part of Ánte that couldn't help hoping. Maybe Erik meant something more.

The hand moved down to Ánte's throat, neck. No way could this be unintentional. Ánte sat totally still. He closed his eyes when Erik moved his fingers to his hair, just inside his hat. Down to his cheek again. When his thumb touched Ánte's lower lip, Ánte had goose bumps all the way down to his boots.

Their eyes met just before Erik let go.

"Your cheeks are getting frostbit," he said, standing. "Let's go back."

It took a while for Ánte's brain to connect with his muscles.

When he stood up, he stumbled in the snow. Erik lifted the reindeer pelt, shook it, rolled it up.

They started walking in silence. Ánte looked at Erik's back, the folds in his brown coat. Wondered whether he would be able to feel the heat from Erik's skin through the thick material if he put his hand there.

Erik turned around.

"I can't see you when you walk back there."

He slowed down, waited for Ánte until they were walking side by side.

A thousand words soared between them, but Ánte didn't know how to take them in his mouth.

His body was still shivering, though he could no longer feel the cold. The heat from Erik's hand was still there inside of him. It felt as if it would never go away.

He turned his face to the sky. Up above, the hunter was tightening his bowstring.

"ÁNTE," HIS DAD called from the hallway.

Cold air spread across the floor. Even though an entire day had gone by since Erik touched him, he could still feel Erik on his skin.

"What?"

"Can you come outside and help me with something?"

His dad stomped off the porch, leaving the door ajar. Ánte closed it, then put his winter clothes on. They were cold against his skin.

Outside, around the corner, the forest stood silent. Black bark, dark trunks, white ground. The sky had turned a coral hue. The light was burrowing into the earth.

Ánte's dad stood next to a big burlap sack. He nodded toward the sled that he had hooked up to the snowmobile.

"My back can't handle this," he said, making a face that was all too easy to interpret. "Can you do it?"

Ánte lifted. His muscles strained. The sack landed on the sled with a thud, the logs in the bag clattering against one another.

His dad put a hand on his shoulder.

"We're lucky to have you young people. Your old dad would never make it without you, you know."

Ánte felt his dad's fingers through the fabric of his coat. He remembered when his hand had been tiny in his dad's big one. He had stretched his fingers out as wide as they would go but they had still not reached beyond the palm of his dad's hand. Back then Ánte's thumb had been thinner than his dad's little finger.

Dad's nails were wide and flat, short. He cut them with regular scissors. In the summer he would sit on the porch outside the house and cut, let the clippings disappear in the grass next to him. Sometimes he would sing. Sometimes he even yoiked. But it had been a long time now.

Ánte's hands were still thin, not rough enough. His shoulder felt cold when his dad let go. As if something had been there that was now missing.

"You went out to the reindeer this morning, right?" his father asked.

Ánte nodded, his head bent. No matter how much he tried, it was impossible to see each individual snowflake, all he could see was a blanket of white.

"These," his father continued, "are our roots."

Ánte wasn't sure if his dad was looking at the snowmobile and the sack of firewood, the reindeer pasture, the land or the forest off in the distance. Maybe it didn't matter. His dad's breath was warm in the winter air. It reached all the way to Ánte's face.

"And roots can never be destroyed."

WHEN THEY GOT inside the house, it looked pitch-black outside. His dad took a can from the refrigerator, opened it with a click and filled his glass. The beer fizzed and foamed.

"Want some?" he asked.

Ánte raised his eyebrows.

"I'm sixteen."

"And soon you'll be as old as me. You wait. It's just a matter of time before little mini-Ántes run around here calling me Áddjá."

"I don't know about that."

They sat down in the living room—his dad with a glass of beer, Ánte without. His mother was sitting on the corner couch with a red knitting project in her hands. She freed one hand when Ánte sat down next to her, stroked his cheek with the back of her hand. He made a face, picked up a pillow to lean his chin on.

"You're my child," she said. "I should get to touch you."

Ánte's dad turned on TV3. The first thing you saw was two guys. Two guys kissing. One was pushing against the other, tugging at his shirt, his hands creeping in under it.

Ánte stopped breathing. Hugged the pillow closer to his body.

"Bloody hell," his dad said. "Can't believe they show this stuff on television."

His mom looked up from her knitting, shook her head.

His dad reached for the remote and changed the station. Bombs were exploding on the screen; little men running through a gray landscape. They looked like tin soldiers. The world was on fire.

"Do we have anything for lunch tomorrow?" his mom asked.

"There's some palt left," his dad said.

She nodded and looked at Ánte.

"What do you want to watch?"

He shrugged.

"Nothing."

His dad was slouching, his legs on the couch. Ánte could see the mirror image of the explosions in his eyes. Tiny little fires.

"See if you can find something," his mom said.

Ánte picked up his phone and looked for a TV guide. He held the screen close to his face, looked for TV3. An American romantic drama had started at eight. When he clicked on the title the two guys appeared on the screen. According to the description, the movie was about a young man who left his bride-to-be for the love of his life, a love interest that he had tried to resist for a long time.

Ánte put his phone down and shook his head.

"I think I'm going to bed."

"Are you tired already?"

"A little. And I have something to turn in on Monday."

His mom put her hand on his upper arm. Rubbed the fabric of his shirt gently with her thumb.

"Good luck," she said. "My smart guy."

He stood up and looked at his dad, but his dad's eyes were glued to the television. The sound of shooting boomed through the room. His mom picked up the remote and turned the volume down a little.

"Well, good night," Ánte said.

"Night night," his mom said.

His dad mumbled something.

A dab of toothpaste on his shirt. Ánte brushed quickly, spit in the sink after a few seconds. He shoved the toothbrush too far back. He gagged, but nothing came up.

The floor creaked when he walked into his room. He sat down on his bed, turned on the bedside lamp, took out his computer and put it in his lap, tried to find the right streaming service. He scrolled until he saw the guys in a tiny frame. Their faces inches from each other.

He put his headphones on and leaned against the wall.

The movie began. The screen was bright, the music cheerful, happy. It made him jumpy, in a good way.

He heard his mom and dad go to bed. He crept in under the covers, lay on his side and continued watching the movie. The main character had broken up with his fiancée and gone with the other guy.

A door slammed shut behind them. One guy pushed the other one against the wall, shoved him up against the wallpaper, his lips so close, yet so far from the other guy's face that it looked like it must hurt. Slowly, he moved his finger along the waist of the other guy.

Ánte's pillowcase got damp under the corner of his mouth. He tried to wipe it off, but there was still a wet spot. He closed his mouth. Bit his lip.

The guys were on top of each other, around each other, inside each other. When the movie was over, Ánte pushed the computer away and rolled over on his back.

A new feeling settled in behind his rib cage. Something he had never felt before. As if he were floating, just above the mattress. As if he were light and thin. As if anybody could lift him.

Maybe it was possible to live like the guys in the movie.

Maybe Erik could be with Ánte instead of Julia.

His skin tingled, his brain was wide awake. He picked up the phone from his bedside table and found a picture of Erik. A picture where Erik was laughing, showing the creases by the corners of his mouth. The picture was a little blurred. Erik and the photographer had both been moving.

He thought about how Erik's hand had felt against his cheek, his neck, Erik's fingers in his hair. What if Erik wanted the same thing he wanted? The thought sent shivers down his spine.

He stayed like that for a long time, the picture in front of his eyes. His phone began to feel heavy, his fingers softened. He could no longer keep his eyes open.

The feeling glowed inside him until he fell asleep.

A COOL HAND on his forehead. It moved a few strands of hair, put them behind his ear.

"Ánte?"

He squinted. The light from the window pierced his eyes. He turned away, grunted.

"You fell asleep with the light on. In your clothes."

He could barely even hear his mom. Sleep weighed him down like a heavy blanket.

"It's almost noon."

Something hard disappeared from under his arm. He was so sleepy he hadn't noticed that it was there until now. The sheet was cool where it had been, the mattress soft. He shifted a little, made himself comfortable again. Pulled the covers over his face.

The mattress sunk down on the left side. Ánte rolled into his mom's back. The contact made him open his eyes.

His mom was holding a phone—his phone. Was that what had been under his arm? Her face was reflected in the screen. She wasn't reading, was she? He flew up and grabbed his phone.

"What the hell are you doing?"

He sank back down on the bed, pulled the phone to his chest. Felt the pounding through the phone.

"It was under your arm," his mom said. "It didn't look very comfortable."

"You can't just take it!"

"I was trying to be nice."

He stared at the ceiling. It was a little bumpy, not smooth. When he was younger, he had seen patterns up there. He remembered some of the images. The family's goahte, where they stayed when they were marking the reindeer; a dog his dad once had. Now he couldn't find them anymore. All he could see was a white surface.

The mattress shifted back when his mom stood up. She shook her head and fixed the hair bun that had come undone.

"How did your homework go?"

"What?"

"You were working on something yesterday that you had to turn in."

"Right. Fine."

"Good," she said.

He wasn't sure she believed him. She might even have sounded a little irritated.

"That's good," she said.

She left the door ajar when she went.

Ánte's clothes were wrinkled. Getting up made him dizzy for a few seconds. He raked a hand through his hair, tried to flatten the creases on his shirt.

He remembered the movie he'd seen. Smiled when the feeling returned. That sense of hope.

He heard men's voices from the kitchen. His dad was sitting at the table with three of his friends. Ánte took a slice of bread from the pantry and buttered it, cut two chunks of Jokkmokk sausage and put them on the bread.

He sat down. His dad looked at him.

"Too late for good morning."

Ánte didn't answer. He bit into his sandwich. One of the men took a gulp of coffee.

"You think he was the one who stole Robert's helmet that one time?"

"Probably. Fucking fruitcake," Ánte's dad said.

A piece of sausage got stuck in Ánte's throat. He coughed. Tore a piece of paper towel and spit the sausage into it.

The others laughed. A booming laughter. Their stomachs bounced, they scratched their beards.

"It's fucking bad," one of them said. "Lucky he doesn't run around in town anymore."

"Unbelievable that he lasted as long as he did," another one laughed.

"What, who?" Ánte asked.

They all looked at him. They didn't seem to have noticed him until now.

"Remember Ruben?" his dad said. "Fucking crazy guy. I think I told you about that one time in the winter when he ran outside in the middle of the night to chop wood? He needed light so he started his snowmobile and almost ran over his wife."

Ánte nodded down at the table.

"But he wasn't gay, was he?"

One of the men shrugged, took a cookie. The others laughed.

"I mean," Ánte said, "if he had a wife."

"That's apparently why he took off," one of his dad's friends said. "He supposedly had an affair with some man during their entire fucking marriage."

"The only reason you'd leave this place would be if you'd done something like that," somebody said. "We have everything here."

"That's right. What do these young people want? Even Lasse left in the end."

Ánte had not thought about Lasse for a long time. When Ánte was a kid Lasse lived in the house across the street. Now it was empty. Even though Lasse was Ánte's godfather they had not been in touch much since the move. Sometimes Ánte would get money for his birthday, maybe a Christmas card now and then. They had talked on the phone but not for a long time. Ánte rarely thought of Lasse these days. He could no longer remember why Lasse moved.

One of the men patted his stomach.

"Lasse couldn't stay away from that broad in Stockholm."

"Knocked her up, didn't he?"

"Nothing wrong with Lasse," Dad said. "But if I saw Ruben out there in the road, I'd have a man-to-man with that idiot."

"You think they'll be back for the wedding in the spring?"

"Lasse might. Would be nice to see the man."

Ánte looked down at the table. He didn't know Ruben at all, but he really missed Lasse. As a kid, he'd run between the houses many times. With Lasse, he'd felt older. Braver. With him he wasn't just a kid—he was a friend. Somebody you could talk things over with.

"But if Ruben shows up, I don't know what the hell I'll do."

Ánte's dad shook his head. Red fingers encircled the coffee cup.

"Good thing he wasn't a member of our Sámi village."

"I'll tell you," said one of the men, leaning across the table, "if there had been gays in our village, I would have known it. In fifty-five years, I've not met a single fucker."

Ánte stood up, took a glass from the cupboard above the sink and opened the tap. Water thundered down into the metal drain. It was so loud that it drowned the voices of his dad and his dad's friends. He stuck his finger in the water. Tepid.

His mom came into the kitchen, glanced at him.

"We've already had lunch," she said. "There's still some palt in the refrigerator if you want some."

"Maybe later."

"By the way, can you take care of the reindeer tonight? Your father and I thought we'd go and pick more lichen."

"Sure."

Ánte filled his glass with water and drank it standing up. Then he went to the table, swept up the bread crumbs and dropped them in the trash bin. The men's laughter followed him all the way to his room.

He sat down on his desk chair, spun it around a few times with his foot. The feeling from yesterday had shifted now. He thought about the movie again. Americans. They could do what they wanted. It didn't feel possible for Ánte to live like they lived, no matter how Erik felt. It just wasn't. Dad and Dad's friends had made that more than clear with their opinions. Everything was different here.

What if they would talk about Ánte the way they talked about Ruben? He couldn't risk that.

He found the picture of Erik again. He got a lump in his throat looking at Erik's smile. His finger paused at the right-hand corner of his phone. He looked right into Erik's eyes when he clicked Delete.

IT HAD TURNED dark outside. Ánte wrestled a headlamp down over his hat as he walked toward the shed. On the floor inside the door stood some large white sacks. He pulled two ICA Rajden grocery bags from his pocket and began filling them with lichen.

The reindeer were far away in the pasture. Some were hiding among the sparse trees, others had not yet noticed him. A few were moving closer.

He took some lichen from the bag and spread it on the ground. The reindeer closest to him hurried over and snapped up the little tufts from the snow. He tried to get the ones looking at him from far away to come closer. One of Ida's females startled, making the reindeer nearby dash off to the side.

The rest of the reindeer had gotten used to him by now. They came close, shoved their muzzles against the full plastic bag. A white reindeer tried to put its head between the handles of the bag.

"Hey, you," Ánte said, taking out a fistful of lichen that disappeared into the reindeer's mouth. He spread the rest across the snow. The reindeer flocked around the pile.

He went and sat down by a tree, leaned his head against the trunk and trained his headlamp at the reindeer so he could watch them eat. The sound of their clicking hooves was relaxing. A lullaby.

His hat made a rustling sound against the bark of the pine tree. The snow was beginning to feel hard, dampness making its way through his snow pants. The cold stung his cheeks. At night the whole forest was icy cold—only the reindeer were warm.

When they had eaten almost all the lichen, the white reindeer came up to him. It sniffed the ground, nuzzled his boot.

He trained his headlamp on it.

"How about that," he said when he noticed his own mark in its ears. "Dån la ham muv."

The reindeer ignored him. It came closer, bumped the empty bags in his hands. He shook his head.

"Guorranam li."

The reindeer kept sniffing his glove, not looking at him. He looked at the earmark again. He was used to seeing it from far away, this mark that he would cut into the untouched ears in the summer.

His dad was the one who had taught him how to earmark when he was still a kid. He remembered the warm blood running over his hands, hands previously unsoiled. It was difficult to get the angle of the knife just right, to make the biehkke round enough; it took much longer than it did for his dad. He had practiced at home, of course, on bark, on orange peels, but those never felt like a calf's ear. The ear was much softer, less sturdy, warmer. The animal would lie there between his legs, breathing. His dad would hold the muzzle of the calf while Ánte marked it, guiding him as best he could with his voice. Now and then the calf would move its head and every time, Ánte would get jumpy. When they were finally done, the mark never looked exactly like it should, but he was still proud. His dad was too, he could tell. *You can see whose calf this is,* he'd say. That's what mattered. And Ánte would get to practice marking his calves many times.

Now he tried to make eye contact with the reindeer in front of him. Its eyes were deep, dark. Like glass beads. He reached around the trunk and found some lichen on the other side of the tree. Pulled his glove off and picked up a tuft. His fingers stiffened.

"Dála oattjo," he said, holding his hand out. The reindeer took a few steps forward, sniffed the lichen before it started eating. The muzzle was warm against the palm of his hand.

When he looked at his reindeer he thought of Lasse. And the move.

Ánte would never move, no matter what. If he had to choose, he would choose this. This was where he wanted to be. Always.

"How amazing that you're mine," he whispered, his words thin and fragile. "But when I'm with you, I can't be myself."

But it didn't really matter—because Erik had Julia. The reindeer were more important. The most important. He would not let go of them.

His feelings would probably go away eventually.

With his free hand he reached for the reindeer's forehead. Touched it gently, carefully. As soon as the tips of his fingers stroked the fur, the reindeer tossed its head back. It backed up a few steps, left a dampness in the palm of his hand. The light from his headlamp glimmered in the beady eyes. Ánte saw himself in them, a mirror image. Or maybe it was just his imagination.

THE BOOK WAS HIDDEN in his dresser drawer. The afternoon sun lit up the dust on top of the dresser. White dots danced in the air. The wood squeaked and creaked when he opened the drawer. Then he was holding it in his hands. Didn't want anybody to come in and see it, didn't know what he would say if somebody asked about it. He took off the dust jacket—the soft covers of the book were beige underneath. He looked at the dust jacket in his hand, at the picture of the old man. Then he folded the paper into a tiny parcel, traced the edges with his fingertips. For a moment he held the parcel in his hand. A dark eye stared up at him. Then he threw it toward the trash can in the other corner of the room, causing a sudden inhalation of the plastic bag when the dust jacket landed inside.

He didn't want to look at the book anymore. At least not the pages he'd already seen. But he still wished to find something else in there, something other than the darkness and the horror. It no longer felt like buying the book had been an accident. It felt like he was supposed to read it.

He sat down at the desk and opened the book. It opened to the last spread he had seen, as if the book had been waiting for this. Oh, those faces. All these faces, entirely nameless.

All that was listed under the pictures were numbers and race.

At first, Ánte didn't understand why he recognized one of the men in the collection. *North Bothnian Laplander of mixed race, minus variant,* said the caption beneath the photograph. It wasn't until he saw the woman on the following page that he understood. It was the couple from the picture with Harald Lundgren, the first picture he'd seen. *Anta and Sigga.*

The words crawled along his spine. *Minus variant.* Was this his history? It didn't feel like it. He couldn't see himself in the pictures, couldn't find a common thread. He didn't want to be a part of it—it was too heavy a legacy to carry—but at the same time he did. Because who else was he?

An outsider. Somebody who didn't belong.

A sudden ringtone made him slam the book shut on top of the table. He retrieved his phone. Froze when he saw the name lighting up the display on Facebook Messenger.

He couldn't remember Erik ever calling him before. Maybe when they were kids. He didn't know what to do. He looked around the room, out the window. Was somebody playing a trick on him? Everything looked normal: some clothes strewn across the bedspread; on his desk, homework papers and the book. Next to his bed, the clock was ticking. The only thing that was different was that Erik's name was lighting up his phone, that Erik's voice was only the push of a button away.

But he couldn't very well answer. And he couldn't very well not.

His thumb hovered over the image of the green telephone. Just when he was about to touch it, it stopped ringing. A message: *Erik. Missed call.* The screen turned dark.

He spun around in his chair and stared at the plant that his mom had put on top of the dresser. It was starting to lose its leaves. He looked at the clock, allowed it to keep ticking for another minute. He could wait one more.

Never had a minute felt longer. When the clock said seven after, he opened the message field to type.

Ánte: *Saw you called, what's up?*

He tried adding an emoji, but it felt wrong. The smile was stiff. Besides, he shouldn't look happy: he'd just missed a phone call from Erik. Or should he? Erik had called, after all, even if Ánte didn't know why.

They had not talked about what happened at the lake. Maybe that's why Erik called? But there was really nothing to talk about. Erik had probably just tried to help Ánte stay warm. Or?

A tiny bubble with Erik's face popped up next to Ánte's message. Ánte closed the chat. Erik had read it. He didn't want to be there when the answer came. As if he was just waiting, as if he was eager.

He watched the screen. He wouldn't unlock it until it lit up by itself. He was in no hurry. He made a fist, tried to force his hand to be still, but it wouldn't listen to him.

The screen lit up next to his hand.

Erik: *Nothing, heard back from Máhttu.*

Nothing. In this case, *nothing* could be anything, except the evening at the lake. He was both relieved and disappointed. Maybe it had to do with school if Máhttu could reply.

Ánte regretted it now. He should have replied right away. He didn't want the conversation to end, not now when Erik was so close. Now when he had a reason to text.

Okay, great, he wrote, deleted. Not good.

Ánte: *Ah, ok.*

He paused. It needed something else, something that would make Erik keep texting.

Ánte: *Maybe you need another answer, so you know Máhttu isn't tricking you?*

He added an emoji with its tongue out so Erik would understand that he was joking, but as soon as he sent it, he realized how sad the eyes looked compared with the mouth. Totally brain-dead. The tongue just hung there.

Once again, he put the phone down and turned off the screen. Spun around in his chair. Stuck his tongue out to see how it felt. It wasn't funny at all. Nothing funny about it. Did anybody ever do that in real life?

Then he unlocked his phone even though he wasn't going to. Maybe Erik had replied and he had missed it. But no. The bubble with Erik's picture was at the bottom of the conversation he had already read. *Active 9 minutes ago,* it said under Erik's name.

Then. Bing. His heart reacted before his eyes did. It wasn't Erik, but Ida.

Ida: *Just found a picture of you.*

She sent a meme with a photo of a black dog; its eyes were wide open, showing the white of the eye. Above, it said, *When someone calls you instead of just texting.*

Ánte: *How did you know?*

Ida: *Hard to miss that you hate talking on the phone. You freak out whenever you hear a ringtone . . .*

Ánte: *But, like, that somebody called me just now.*

Ida: *Haha, for real? Maybe I have ESP.*

He looked at the picture one more time. Felt a little calmer for some reason. There was at least someone out there in the world who felt like him.

Erik was still not active in the chat. Maybe he was just busy. Ánte waited all afternoon but no message came from Erik. Why was he acting like this? It wasn't like Erik to totally ignore him. Was he embarrassed about what had happened at the lake? Of course not. Because nothing had happened, not really. It just felt like it.

It *really* felt like it.

He couldn't stand waiting any longer, needed a distraction. Something louder than the buzzing in his head. He opened the chat again and wrote to Ida.

Ánte: *Want to come over?*

She was there before he could even read her reply.

IDA SAT DOWN on Ánte's desk chair and threw her feet up on the desk. She was wearing red wool socks with cartoon characters.

"What are you reading?" she asked, grabbing the book.

"A book," he said. He should have put it back in the dresser drawer.

He lay down on the bed, one arm under his head.

"Geez, but aren't you a chatterbox." Ida opened the book in front of her. A wrinkle appeared above her nose. "Where did you find this?"

"At the market."

She kept flipping through it.

"It's really sick," she said. "What a disgusting old man!"

Ida imitated Harald Lundgren's stern mouth and lowered eyebrows. She actually looked a lot like him.

"Only the glasses missing," she said. "Who called you anyway?"

He hesitated. Something about Ida always made him say more than he had planned.

"Erik."

"Ah," she said. "What did he want?"

"Nothing. Or, he didn't say."

"He called you but didn't say anything . . . ?"

Ánte avoided looking at Ida's eyes. She sighed.

"You seriously didn't answer?"

"I never do."

"Um, I guess not. Does that mean you haven't talked to Hanna?"

"Why would I?"

Ida shrugged. Raised her eyebrows and smiled with exaggerated innocence.

"Just thought she might have checked in with you."

He shook his head. Noticed that he was biting his lip. Couldn't help asking.

"No, but . . . ?"

"Umm?"

"You know Julia a little, don't you? Erik's Julia."

Ida looked at him, quizzically, put her feet on the floor.

"Yes?"

"You know if she . . . Do you, um, know anything about their relationship?"

She snorted.

"That's probably the strangest thing you've ever asked me."

Ánte pinched his lips together, felt his face heat up. It was probably the strangest question he had asked *anybody* ever. Why was it that whenever he said something, it came out all wrong?

"I guess you have to ask Erik. You know him better than I know Julia."

"Nah, it's not important."

Ida's eyes opened wide.

"Wait," she said. "You like Julia? I did *not* see that coming."

His face felt like it had caught on fire. He didn't want to know how he looked.

"No, well, you know . . . Aw . . . just forget it."

Ida shook her head a little and picked up the book again. Was she smiling? He was surprised that she didn't say anything else. She flipped through a few pages, stopped at the photo of Harald Lundgren with the two Sámis.

"Isn't this our village?" She held up the book so he could see. "Near my house?"

"Is it really?"

"Look at the background."

Behind the people was a forest in autumn shroud. Next to it, a lake.

"I recognize the lake," he said. "I think."

"Exactly!"

Ida jumped up from the chair and slid to the door on her socks. She grabbed the doorknob.

"Come on!"

"Where are you going?"

"*We*," she said, "are going to find the place where this photo was taken."

IT WAS DARK OUTSIDE. The lake was frozen, nature buried under snow. The thin birch trees bowed to the ground that was covered in a blanket of heavy snow. Their necks were so bent they looked like they might snap. They looked like they were in mourning. Ánte wondered how long they would be able to stand like that.

Neither one of them said anything. They just stood there, waiting. Ánte closed his eyes, tried to imagine that he was somebody else, somebody who lived a long, long time ago.

It didn't work. Nothing happened, nothing felt different. He felt uncertain about what Ida might have expected. Why were they even here?

It was impossible to recognize the place from the photo. That had been another world. Now everything was hidden or forgotten. The tracks, the memories. Gone.

Ida was the first to turn and leave.

THE SUN WAS SHINING through the pool windows, reflecting off the surface of the water. The light painted patterns on the bottom of the pool. Erik's back gleamed beneath the surface. Skin, water, light. The floor was hard and slippery under Ánte's feet. Goose bumps. He walked closer to the edge.

And jumped.

The pool swallowed him; his hair swirled around his face. He pulled himself up to the surface, snorted, sprayed water from his nose. A strong smell of chlorine.

The teacher's voice echoed in the swimming hall.

"Breaststroke eight laps, then eight laps backstroke!"

Ánte took a few strokes, sucked in air, moved slower than the rest. He couldn't find the right technique. He saw Erik turn onto his back and start swimming in the opposite direction. Chest and stomach shining in the sun. Ánte closed his eyes. He inhaled suddenly, cold water burning his nose.

Something bumped his feet, made his legs sink.

"Oops, sorry!" Erik said.

He was breathing fast, smiled at Ánte, showing his teeth.

Ánte floated on his back again. The surface of the water gently touched the sides of his legs, lapped at his waist.

"No problem," Ánte said, but Erik was already gone.

Ánte had several laps of breaststroke left but he stayed on his back, allowing his body to rest in the space between water and air. The light blinded him, warmed his face through the glass window.

What was happening? His body seemed to have quit working. Again and again, his nose almost dipped under the surface. Erik caught up with him before Ánte had even made a full lap around the pool. He wanted to reach out, touch Erik's fingers with his own.

His fingertips had already gotten wrinkled, like raisins.

He tipped his head to see if he was swimming too close to Erik. Didn't want to risk a collision. But his movement was too sudden for the surface to hold him. The water lost its grip.

A hand under his back.

"Like this," Erik said, pushing him to the surface.

Ánte weighed nothing in the water. Erik touched him as if it didn't mean anything. Again.

"Relax a little."

Not a single muscle relaxed. What if somebody saw them? Ánte told his head to lean back, told his legs to let go. A breathtaking feeling.

"You see? If you just relax, you'll float."

Ánte's breathing slowed. He counted Erik's five fingers on his skin over and over and over. Stared up at the ceiling. The lights had turned into bubbles and he closed his eyes, let go of all thoughts.

He was floating in Erik's hand.

THE SMELL OF BODIES and shampoo wafted out through the door as the guys made their way into the changing room. Moisture clung to their skin. A cold arm on Ánte's back, wet swim trunks brushing against hips. Ánte shoved his way past, shrugged off the feeling.

Erik was about to take a shower farther in. He was pulling his trunks off, wringing the water out. Ánte stared at the ceiling, clenched his jaw. A current coursed through his blood, but his skin was cool. He stepped into the first available shower stall. The shower turned on automatically, hot rays burning his skin. He stared at the wall. Tried to think of anything but Erik. Sports. Snowmobiles. War. Horrible, disgusting, ugly fish.

Ánte showered with his trunks on. He squeezed soap from a container on the wall and lathered his body. Massaged a dollop into his hair. He rinsed quickly, hurried across the slippery floor. Wrapped the towel around himself and pulled his wet trunks off.

Erik stepped out of the shower stall. He shook his head, making droplets of water splash over his shoulders. Shiny beads on his belly. Wet hair stuck to his face. He rubbed a pale blue terrycloth towel over his hair until it stood out in every direction. Ánte shivered, gripped his own towel tightly around his waist, made his eyes stop at Erik's belly button, did not allow them to look even a centimeter farther down.

The chill from the changing room hit him like a wall when he opened the door. Erik was behind him, raised his foot and pulled off the rubber band with the key. Opened the locker. Ánte picked up his own key, which he had placed on top of Erik's clothes.

Erik's underwear clung tightly to his wet skin. Here and there, you could see through the white material. Ánte sat down on the bench. He still wore the towel around his waist. Erik had started pulling his jeans on. His zipper was down, his chest bare. He walked up to a large mirror, brushed his hair from his face.

Ánte pulled his boxers on under the towel. Erik started buttoning his red plaid shirt. In his mind, Ánte unbuttoned every button again. Pinched his own hand hard.

He wrestled his T-shirt down over his head and smeared a layer of deodorant in his armpits. His hair was still damp. His jeans protested when he pulled them on.

"Are you coming?"

Erik had already zipped his coat. He stepped into his shoes and tied them. Ánte moved quickly, got his coat on as fast as he could. It clung to his body but left a gap at his waist. The lining of the coat was soft against the strip of skin that was exposed.

Outside, the snow squeaked beneath their shoes. The sun created a million tiny stars in the sea of white. Erik's hair turned into nails. When he opened his mouth, you could see his breath, like smoke.

"When does the bus leave for the village?"

"In like three minutes," Ánte answered.

Erik laughed.

"What could the girls possibly be doing in the changing room for so long? They always miss the bus."

Ánte shook his head, shivering inside his coat. Why did Erik talk about the girls now, when they had not yet talked about the most important thing? Like why Erik had called and then not answered Ánte's message, for example. He had to ask.

"No idea, but um . . . ?"

"Yeah?"

"What did you want when you called?"

Erik raised his eyebrows a tiny bit.

"Nothing, I told you."

Maybe Ánte would never know. He hoped that his disappointment was not too apparent.

When they reached the bus stop, some people from their class were already there. Ida was the only girl. She looked at Ánte and Erik, smiled a little too much.

"Where are your friends?" Erik asked.

Ida pretended to be insulted. Ánte didn't even have to pretend.

"You're my friends," she said.

"Yeah, but the girls."

She looked mischievous.

"You think I'd tell you? You, our worst rivals?"

"No need." Juhán looked up from his phone, winked. "Erik and I already know all your secrets."

The bus stopped in front of them and suddenly the boys were in a hurry. Ánte and Ida got on last. Heat surrounded him when he stepped onto the bus.

Juhán had grabbed the seat next to Erik. Ánte sat down behind them and leaned in between their seats.

"What did you even mean by that?"

Juhán was looking at his phone when he answered.

"What?"

"It's not like you've been in the girls' locker rooms."

"No." He grinned. "But unlike some people, we know a little something about these ladies."

Ida threw her bag in Ánte's lap and sat down next to him.

Her hair was dark and wet. It smelled like watermelon. The frozen tips had started to thaw from the warm air from the fan.

Juhán showed Erik a video clip on his phone. They laughed. Ánte waited for Juhán to turn the screen in his direction, but he didn't.

Ánte sank back in his seat and leaned his head against the frozen windowpane. The rocking of the bus made him sleepy. He could see Erik's reflection in the bus window.

Ida put her head on Ánte's shoulder. His neck got a little damp. She turned and came even closer and whispered:

"It's strange that so much can happen in a place and you can't even tell."

He tried to see her face but couldn't.

"What do you mean?"

"Everything that happens leaves traces. Why weren't there any?"

He remembered the lake and the birch trees, weighed down by snow.

"Maybe because it's winter," he said. "Winter makes you forget everything that's been there before."

"True," Ida said. "Let's wait until spring."

ÁNTE'S BED CREAKED when he sat up. He brought his hands to his heart; it went boom, boom, boom inside.

His pulse refused to slow down. His covers were warm and damp across his legs, his tongue felt like a rock in his mouth. He kept one hand on his chest, tried to breathe more slowly, make his heart follow suit. Eventually, it began to calm down.

He turned his bedside lamp on and sank back. It felt like his mattress was thrumming beneath him. A strong sense of discomfort lingered in his chest.

When he closed his eyes, pictures from his dream returned. Erik's dark eyes. Mean laughter. An incessant chatter. It had been a dream but it felt so real. He needed to see Erik in real life, talk to him. Make sure everything was all right.

MÁHTTU WAS AT THE BUS STOP. His legs were moving restlessly, he was stomping with one foot. Looked up from his phone, waved when he saw Ánte.

"Hey."

The bus would be there in a few minutes. Ánte looked down the road, in the direction that Erik usually came from. The road was still and empty, bumpy from the snow and ice. A figure came toward them over the hill. Ánte squinted to see better. When the person got closer, he saw that it was an older woman with a dog on a leash. She raised her hand. He waved back.

"Have you heard from Erik?"

Máhttu shrugged.

"What do you mean heard?"

"Well, the bus will be here soon."

Máhttu smiled and squinted at Ánte. Scraped the ground with one foot, swept some gravel off the ice. Tiny rocks rolled toward Ánte's feet.

"Has the bus ever been on time?"

"Maybe he won't make it."

"The bus?"

Ánte frowned.

"No, Erik."

A white cloud materialized when Máhttu let the air out of his lungs. It looked like he was smoking.

"He'll probably be here soon."

The bus drove up the slope. Ánte put his hand in his pocket and pulled out his bus pass. Maybe Erik had been delayed. Should he ask the bus driver to wait? Or should he call Erik? He let Máhttu get on the bus first, then a few girls from school. They looked at him with a puzzled expression when he threw a last glance down the road. Still white and empty.

He got on the bus.

Máhttu had taken a seat for four people and put his feet up on the seat next to him. Ánte sat down across from him and took out his phone. He should text Erik that the bus was leaving. So he knew. In case he was wondering.

"What's going on?" Máhttu asked.

Ánte looked up. He clutched his phone.

"Nothing."

"Sure?"

"Just wondering where Erik is."

"Ah."

Máhttu leaned toward the window, his hat against the pane. One of his feet was still jerking, it kept bumping the seat.

"He doesn't usually skip school," Ánte said.

"He's probably sick or something."

"Wouldn't he have mentioned it if he was sick?"

Máhttu's foot stopped. He moved his legs off the seat, put both feet on the floor and leaned toward Ánte. A tiny smile in the corner of his mouth.

"Now you have to tell me."

"What?"

"Something's obviously going on."

Ánte shrugged, sank deeper into his seat. Hadn't noticed until now that he'd been super tense. "Don't I get to wonder?"

"Well, you're not wondering where Juhán is."

Ánte sighed.

"He's not usually here."

"I think Erik can take care of himself."

Ánte looked at the floor of the bus, at Máhttu's feet, which were no longer moving. The picture of dream-Erik was still on his retina. But it was more of a feeling than a picture, really—a discomfort that refused to let go. He tried to shake it off.

"Whatever. Just wondering."

"Uh-huh."

Máhttu put his feet up again. His shoes left dirt on the seat. Not that Ánte cared. He just needed something to focus on.

"Just had a weird dream."

"About what?"

"Hard to remember."

"Now you'll have to tell me!"

"Something to do with Erik. But he wasn't himself. Or, well, I don't know."

Máhttu laughed out loud. Ánte closed his mouth, tight. Why was he even telling him this? It wasn't supposed to be funny. Dreams always sounded different when you talked about them. It was impossible to even describe the feeling.

"What was he doing?"

"Nah, forget it."

Máhttu was still chuckling.

"What did you drink before you fell asleep?"

Ánte scoffed.

"Nothing."

"Is that why you're acting so funny?"

Ánte shook his head, looked at the trees outside the window.

"Who's talking, weirdo."

THEY WALKED FROM THE BUS STOP. As they neared the school, they saw Erik and Juhán walking toward the front door. Máhttu pointed.

"There you go. They're alive and kicking."

Ánte tried to walk matching Máhttu's steps, keep his feet from running. Why had Erik and Juhán not been on the bus?

His breathing was heavy from the cold. When they got inside the school building, he was panting. His toes felt like lumps of ice in his shoes.

Erik and Juhán were standing by the lockers.

"Hey," Ánte said.

"But the new version is better," Erik said. He took out his computer. "At least it doesn't have that same twisted view on women."

"Whatever," Juhán said. "The original is a fucking masterpiece. We're talking classic."

"I guess. But it hasn't aged well."

"What?" Juhán raised his voice a little. "There's just as much violence against men. You mean you get to murder men but not women?"

Erik slammed his locker shut.

"Don't want to talk about this anymore."

"Hi there," Ánte said. He made eye contact for a moment before Erik looked away. "How did you get here?"

"Got a ride with Juhán's mom. She was on her way to work."

Ánte opened his locker, pretended to be looking for something deep inside. Didn't want them to see his face. He traced the outline of his math book with his finger. Put it to where the Swedish book had been.

"Um-hum," he said.

"Ánte thought you'd been kidnapped or something," he heard Máhttu say. "He was really funny."

Erik let out a forced laugh. Juhán tapped his pencil against Ánte's locker.

"What about me? Nobody wondered if I had been kidnapped?"

Ánte forced himself to come out of the locker, shut it.

"Nope," Máhttu said. "He said you miss school all the time."

Juhán looked at Ánte. "At least I know I don't have to come looking for you next time you disappear," he said.

"*Next* time?" Ánte asked.

"Didn't think we had to announce everything we did to you," Erik said.

Ánte stood quietly with his computer and his books in his arms. Picked at the edge of the binder with his thumbnail. It felt strange to see Erik after the dream. The feeling refused to let go.

"That's what I said," said Máhttu. "But he'd had some dream that got him all worked up."

"What kind of dream?" Erik asked.

"About you, probably," Juhán said.

Erik showed no reaction to these words.

"Tell them," Máhttu said.

Ánte shot him a glance that made him shut up. Máhttu shook his head almost imperceptibly.

"Oh well." Máhttu turned to the others. "Class is starting."

Ánte left without checking to see if the others were behind him. His face was hot. It would be best if he never spoke again. Shut up for the rest of his life.

THE BUZZING FROM the cafeteria surrounded Ánte where he stood in line behind Erik. It was crowded. He tried to keep a reasonable distance, but Juhán and Máhttu were pushing from behind. He could feel the heat from Erik's back, looked at the tiny hairs on his neck, lighter than his skin.

Ánte loaded potatoes onto his plate. And a light gray piece of fish of unknown origin. A dab of cold sauce spread over the porcelain, mixing with some shredded carrots.

Erik was already sitting at the table when Ánte got there. Unless somebody else got there before them, they always sat in the same spot. Whenever their table was taken, they were lost in the cafeteria. Like strangers in their own home.

He sat down across from Erik. A little milk splashed on the table.

Erik looked up, handed him a napkin.

"Here."

Their fingers touched when Ánte took it.

When Erik looked away, Ánte put the napkin in his pocket. He used his plate to cover the spill.

Juhán and Máhttu's arrival was impossible to miss. Chairs scraping, silverware clinking against the table. Juhán laughed out loud at something, his face shiny. He sat down next to Erik.

Máhttu took the last seat, his elbow bumping Ánte's shoulder.

"Is it any good?"

Ánte shrugged. Stared down at his plate, cut a potato in two. It was white inside.

"Look," Juhán said, his voice low. The whole table looked in the same direction.

A group of girls in black jeans walked toward them. They all wore their long hair down. When they walked by, Ánte saw that one of the girls was Hanna, Ida's friend, the one who had come with them to the market.

Juhán made a hole with his thumb and index finger and stuck two fingers in it. Ánte swallowed.

"Seriously," he said. "Cut it out."

Erik looked at him but it was impossible to read the expression on his face. What was he thinking?

Juhán raised his eyebrows.

"Just because you're such a fucking virgin, Ánte."

Ánte glared at him.

"Who's talking!"

Erik looked like he was trying not to laugh.

"Halfway there," Juhán said. "I've got something going on with Hanna."

Juhán and Hanna? Ida hadn't told him about that.

Ánte was surprised, but also a little relieved. There was something about Hanna that felt a little too intimate. Maybe she was like that with everybody.

"Congratulations," Ánte said.

"Dream on," Máhttu said.

Juhán turned to Erik.

"You get laid yet?"

Erik looked away, smiled stiffly.

"I have a girlfriend," he said finally. "Use your brain."

Ánte's stomach turned inside out. Juhán howled.

"Erik fucking rules," he said, leaning in. "Teach us all you know, Romeo!"

Erik shoved him.

"You're unteachable."

Máhttu shook his head and Juhán sank back in his chair.

Ánte picked at his fish, put some in his mouth.

"But do you think Hanna's cute? The blonde?" Juhán asked.

Erik was quiet, texting. His plate was already empty. He was probably texting with Julia. Ánte touched Erik's fingers with his eyes.

"Not as cute as Ella," Máhttu said.

"Honestly," Juhán said. "Ella's not even cute. I don't get how you can be so hot for her."

"Then there's something wrong with your eyes."

Juhán shrugged.

"Or there's something wrong with your dick."

"Um," Máhttu said. "Were we planning to play FIFA at my house later?"

Juhán looked at Erik, shoved him.

"I think this Romeo is too preoccupied with his Julia."

Erik shook his head and put his phone down.

"I can do it."

Juhán cheered and Máhttu turned to Ánte.

"What about you?"

"Okay," he said. His voice seemed to be coming from far away.

"Cool," Juhán said. "Want to skip English so we can leave early?"

Erik stood up.

"Watch your grades."

"Okay, Mom."

Juhán imitated Erik's voice, spoke loudly, then he threw his silverware on the plate. They sank in the fish sauce.

"Ánte and I will win, hands down."

Erik's words startled Ánte. Why was he saying that? They were never on the same team, because the other two always objected when they were. Erik was right, they *would* win if they were on the same team.

Ánte's fingers closed around the edge of the plate. If he had been stronger, it might have broken.

"No way," Juhán said.

"But seriously," Máhttu said. "It won't even be fun."

"What, too chicken to play us?" Erik said. He looked into Ánte's eyes for such a short moment that Ánte might have imagined it.

Erik winked.

MÁHTTU'S ROOM FELT like a dark cave. It had the sweet smell of sweat. On the small table in front of the TV were a few cans of energy drinks. Cables and controllers fought for space next to the PS4 on the TV bench. Ánte sat down on the leather couch, sank almost to the floor. Juhán sat next to him.

Erik stood for a moment before he sat down right in Juhán's lap.

"Ouch!"

"I want to sit here."

Juhán moved aside and Erik pushed his way in between the two of them. There was barely enough room for him. His thigh pushed against Ánte's, burned through Ánte's jeans. Their shoulders touched. They had never sat this close to each other. Why did Erik want to sit right here? The beanbag chairs next to the couch were available. Ánte picked at the skin by his thumbnail.

"I don't want to be fucking crammed in here with you," Juhán said, standing up.

A big, empty space appeared between Erik and the edge of the couch. But he didn't budge a centimeter. Why didn't he move? It was weird to sit this close. And yet, Ánte wanted him to come even closer.

Juhán sat in one of the beanbag chairs, Máhttu in the other. Máhttu's fingers were moving across his phone.

"Who are you texting?" Juhán asked. "Some chick?"

Máhttu didn't look up.

"Maybe."

"Ella can wait," Juhán said. "Look, Erik's not texting with his girl now that we're doing something more important."

A small crease appeared between Erik's eyebrows. A moment later his face turned neutral again, the wrinkle gone, but not before Ánte had caught it on his retina. Did Erik wish he could be texting with Julia right now?

Maybe he would rather be with her.

Erik put his hand on his thigh. His little finger ended up on Ánte's leg.

"Just chill," Máhttu said, letting his phone slide into the pocket of his sweats. He picked up the controller and began thumping it against his thigh to the beat of the music.

Ánte had a firm hold on his own controller. His thumbs moved across the levers. His awareness of Erik reached out in his very fingertips. He couldn't keep them still.

Juhán picked up his controller and chose *Kick Off*. The soccer arena lit up the room and four digital game controllers popped up in the middle of the screen. Time to pick teams.

Erik was fast. He chose the visitor team, then threw himself on top of Ánte, smashed him against the edge of the couch. Even though Ánte knew what Erik wanted him to do, it was as if his brain had shut down.

"Go ahead already, pick my team!"

He couldn't move. His entire body was throbbing. Erik was covering half of him. Erik grabbed the controller from Ánte's hand and picked the same team.

"What the fuck," Juhán said and moved over to the home team.

Máhttu jumped to Ánte and Erik's team.

Juhán held up his controller.

"Seriously, there can't be three of you!"

"I thought we'd agreed that Ánte and Erik couldn't be on the same team."

"Aw, are you sad?" Erik said.

Máhttu crossed his arms, pretended to pout.

"We'll switch for the next game."

Máhttu changed to Juhán's team.

Laughter bubbled out of Erik's body. You could feel it everywhere. Erik put his cheek on Ánte's shoulder. Ánte forgot to breathe.

"Eww," Juhán said. "You guys."

He waved the controller at the screen and Erik sat up.

"At least we get to be Liverpool," Juhán continued. "You want to be the women's national team then?"

Máhttu laughed so hard that he sank even farther down in the beanbag chair.

"Erika and Anta," he said.

"Anta isn't even a girl's name," Ánte said.

"Let's go with that," Erik said.

Juhán snorted.

"Eh, okay."

He started the game. Passed the ball to Máhttu, who caught it and ran. He moved the ball past one player, then two, then three.

"Pass it!" Juhán yelled.

Máhttu kept dribbling toward the penalty box.

"What the hell, Máhttu. Your controller's not working or what?"

Máhttu mumbled something incomprehensible, started getting up from the beanbag chair.

Erik's face was furrowed with concentration. His fingers were moving smoothly across the buttons. His elbow touched Ánte now and then.

"Stop him," Erik hissed.

Ánte tried and tried but he no longer knew what he was doing. It was as if he had never played before. Juhán and Máhttu were yelling, Erik's body was pushing against his and Ánte was drowning in sweat. The voices turned into a background buzzing. He wanted to throw his controller on the floor, turn to Erik, touch him.

"*Yeeees!*" Juhán yelled when Máhttu scored. "Now what do you say, girls?"

Máhttu stood up and applauded as the commentators cheered at his triumph. Erik pounded his controller against the couch.

"Cut it out already, we don't want to see your goal a million times," he said.

"Oh yeah, check it out," Máhttu said. "It was so fucking awesome."

Ánte stared down in his lap, couldn't help seeing Erik's right knee next to his own left knee. It started to feel unbearable to sit here. He had never played this poorly before, could hardly control his own hands. It felt as if he had let Erik down. He had been so sure that they would win.

The game continued and the only thing Ánte did was run. Every time he got the ball, he passed it to Erik. The rest of the time he stayed in the periphery, followed Erik's movements with the controller. Erik said nothing, tried to do most of the work himself. He was as good as always, but Ánte was not much help.

Máhttu and Juhán won the game. They whooped and hollered and Erik's leg was sweaty against Ánte's and the entire room was sweaty and a thousand birds were flapping around in his stomach.

"Brave enough for a rematch?" Máhttu asked, sinking down in the beanbag chair.

He took a gulp of his energy drink. Erik held back laughter, raised his eyebrows.

"You were just lucky."

Ánte stood up. His thighs were hot, his pants damp with sweat as they came unstuck from the leather upholstery. He couldn't sit there anymore and pretend like nothing was the matter. Soon everybody would start to wonder what was wrong with him.

"I'm heading out."

"What?"

Everybody stared at him.

"I have to go."

The couch squeaked when Erik stood up.

"I'll go with you."

Ánte didn't know what to say so he said: "Okay."

"Noooo," Juhán whined. "You can be Liverpool this time!"

"Sorry," Ánte said. "Have to do something."

"Are you serious?"

"See you tomorrow."

"What the fuck?"

He left the room without looking to see if Erik was behind him.

His lungs needed air. He found his shoes in the entryway and pulled his coat on, stopped on the porch to let the cold air soak into his clothes.

Took a breath in. A breath out.

"How are you?"

Erik stood close to him. Much too close.

"Don't know," Ánte said.

He stepped down in the snow, heard Erik's steps behind him. Why was he following him? Why did he want to be with Ánte when he had Julia? And why did he touch Ánte sometimes, only to pretend later that nothing had happened?

It felt like a single step might make the ground break open.

"I know something's going on."

Ánte hid his hands in his coat pockets, squeezed a coin, a bunched-up receipt. Didn't look behind him when he answered.

"I was just tired."

"Ánte."

Nobody could say his name like Erik.

Ánte stopped. He turned around slowly, and there was Erik's body, so close to his.

"What?"

"Are you getting sick?"

All he could do was nod. Didn't know if he was lying. It was probably true.

"You can take it easy when you get home."

They kept walking. His forehead felt heavy, his skin warm. Maybe he had a fever after all.

"You were pretty off when we played," Erik said. "Otherwise, we would have won easily."

"I know. Maybe I have a fever."

Erik nodded, his head bent. The silence was palpable. Ánte searched for words in his head; there should be something he could say or ask.

"Are you going to be with Julia now?"

Erik looked up.

"Why do you want to know that?"

Ánte shrugged.

"Why did you come with me? You could have stayed and kept playing."

"Maybe I'd rather be with you."

"But most of all with Julia, right?"

Erik laughed.

"What's with you?"

Ánte regretted even opening his mouth. He didn't know what he was doing either. The words just came out.

"What do you want me to say?" Erik said. "That Julia and I are probably about to break up? There you are. Now you know."

The relief. The shameful relief. Ánte tried really hard not to show how he felt.

"What? Did something happen?"

"No, that's the problem. Everything feels so superficial. It's as if she's with me just to look good."

Erik didn't usually talk that much about Julia and their relationship. Ánte didn't know what to say. He only knew that he wasn't supposed to feel the way he felt. He tried to stop a smile from breaking through. Shook his head.

"That's hard," he said.

Erik looked at him, smiled a little.

"Never get a girlfriend," he said. "It makes for a bad story."

"What do you mean?"

"Boy meets girl. You can *never* guess what happens after that."

"What does happen?"

They had reached Ánte's house. He didn't want to go inside yet, stopped on the sidewalk even though the cold bit into his very bones. Erik came close, swept his hand over Ánte's arm. Touched the back of his hand lightly.

Ánte hardly knew what was happening but suddenly Erik was backing away, leaving.

"Get well," he said.

And just like that, the chill was gone.

HE UNFOLDED THE NAPKIN on his bed. The napkin that Erik had handed him in the cafeteria. Was it crazy that he'd saved it? It was small and thin, a white membrane on his sheet. There was nothing there to remind him of Erik, just creases and folded corners. He didn't know what came from his pocket and what came from Erik.

He lay down and picked up the napkin. Looked at it for a long time. Why did he save a napkin? Was there any part of Erik still left on it? Maybe he had gone crazy for real.

The napkin was rough against his face. He tried to feel Erik's fingers through the paper. Thought about how they had felt against his cheek, his arm, thought about Erik's warm thigh against his own. The hand that had grazed his leg.

He pulled his T-shirt up a little, moved the palm of his hand over his jeans. Unbuttoned the button, fought the zipper. His body reacted to the touch. Pounded, throbbed. His skin was warm through the material. His body trembled when he moved. His heart pounded. Hard, hard, hard.

He thought of Erik as his. An Erik who had broken up with Julia, who only wanted to be with him, Ánte. Who touched him on purpose. Of course, it was on purpose.

Erik's fingers on the inside of his thigh. Warm, soft lips. Erik's hand on his chest. His tongue.

Ánte vibrated in his own grip. Moved faster and faster before he spasmed. Then he was overwhelmed with feelings reverberating through his body.

His fingers stuck to one another. He picked up the napkin, which had fallen on his pillow, and wiped his hand brusquely. The paper stuck to his skin.

He pulled out the drawer of his bedside table and put the napkin in it. He lifted his hands to his face. His breath was warm against the palms of his hand. His eyelashes grazed his fingers. He kept his eyes open, looked into the dark space that his hands created. Red, brown, black. He lay like that for a while, waiting for his breath to calm down. It didn't. Instead, his heart started beating harder. Tried to save itself from what was happening in there.

Memory after memory flashed by. His dad's harsh words, the men's mean laughter. What would they say if they knew about Ánte? What he was thinking right now? Maybe it didn't matter if Erik broke up with Julia. Maybe things were still just as impossible.

HIS DAD STUCK HIS HEAD into the living room and nodded to Ánte, who was slumped down on the couch.

"Would you go to Áhkko's and pick up the bread?" he said. "So she won't have to bring it over. It's so darn slippery outside."

Ánte looked up from his phone.

"What bread?"

"She said she was baking for us."

"Why should I go? She said it to you."

His mom put her newspaper down.

"If you have healthy young legs, you should use them."

It was not far to Áhkko's but his dad was right. The roads were icy, not yet sanded. Ánte took tiny steps. This was probably the worst time of the year.

He saw his grandmother's red house in the distance. Her yard was full of things. A snowmobile, a few sacks of pellets, a sled with a tarp over it. He crossed the yard and knocked on the door. Next to the porch was a pile of tangled reindeer antlers.

"Ánndaris!" Áhkko burst out when she opened the door and hugged him.

Her head reached exactly to his shoulder. She grabbed his arms, leaned back and squinted as if it had been years since she last saw him.

"Dån la áhtját muoduk," she said.

"Nah," Ánte said. "Not exactly."

"Spot-on," Áhkko said. "You should have seen him when he was your age. You might have thought it was Anders who came in through that door."

He freed himself from her grip and she waved him inside.

"Boade sisi," she said, backing into the entryway.

He followed behind her, hung his outerwear on a hook. He left his boots right inside the door. Even though Áhkko lived alone, the entryway was full of clothes. Coats, snow pants, overalls. If you needed something, you'd find it there.

He looked at the collage of pictures crammed together in a wooden frame next to the hall mirror. Pictures of Ida on her birthday, Áhkko and Áddjá in Greece in 1982. Áhkko's thin legs in the ocean, Áddjá's arm around her. Little Ánte on Lasse's shoulders, wearing neon pink headphones, a helicopter in the background from the local company Fiskflyg. Ánte smiled at the picture. Felt a sting of longing.

A few of the pictures had started to slide down inside the glass. A black Lapponian Herder dog had slid down from its spot. The dog picture covered Ánte's face in the photo below it. Only his tanned neck and his dark blue gábdde were visible.

"How nice to see you here," Áhkko said. "Well, how are you?"

"Fine," Ánte said. "I was supposed to pick up some bread."

She held up a finger, as if she'd only just remembered. Then she disappeared into the kitchen. After a while she peeked through the door opening. Her white bangs hid her eyebrows, looked like they were getting stuck in her eyelashes.

"Maybe I shouldn't take out the bread just yet, it's in the freezer. That way it won't thaw."

"Okay?"

"You'll stick around for a little while, right?"

His hand crept down in his jean pocket.

"Sure."

"I'm in the living room, making bootlaces. Thought you might need new ones, since Sunná and Stefan are getting married in the spring."

The walls in Áhkko's living room were covered with pictures. The wallpaper with its sun-bleached flowers could be glimpsed only in the gaps between them. Reindeer, mountain landscapes and relatives dressed in gábde. From the radio on the windowsill came the Sámi news. Áhkko turned the volume down until the voices were just a low mumbling.

She picked up a spool, a red and a blue skein of yarn, and sat down on the couch in the corner of the room. Ánte sat at the other end of the couch, watched when she moved the yarn. Her fingers were dry. Looking at them, he remembered how they felt on his skin. Coarse and tender. A light touch on his cheek.

On the coffee table were an envelope and a messy pile of photos. Ánte leaned over and picked through the pictures.

"I'm weeding a little," Áhkko said. "Have to sort through the pictures so it'll be easier to find things."

There was yet another picture of Lasse and Ánte from that same time period. Ánte looked at it for a long time, laughed a little at the pink headphones. They looked so big compared to his head.

Áhkko glanced at him.

"Are you looking at Lasse? He actually called the other day."

"He did?"

Ánte didn't know that Áhkko was in touch with Lasse. Was Ánte the only one who barely knew him anymore? He couldn't help feeling disappointed. Wished Lasse would have called him some time too.

"What did you talk about?"

"This and that. He seems to really like Stockholm."

Ánte nodded.

"I haven't seen him for a long time."

He pulled out a small, square photo with soft edges. It showed a girl with long, dark braids. Behind her, the mountains. Everywhere.

"Who is this?"

"It's me," Áhkko said. "Don't know how old I might have been. Maybe six, seven."

He looked at the girl, then at his áhkko. At the wrinkles on her forehead. The dark spot by one of her cheekbones. The skin that looked so thin by the corner of her eye. It was hard to understand that she was the same person as the girl in the photo. That she had once been so young.

The room turned quiet. At Áhkko's, silence felt safe. A low yoik came from the radio, a soft ticking sound from the clock in the bedroom. It was the kind of silence that you could rest inside.

Ánte kept looking at the pictures. There was an entire envelope with photos in the same style. He recognized one of the men but could not put his finger on who it was. His face was marked by years of labor.

"That was my grandfather, Ánnda. You were named after him. Anders too, of course."

He recognized the name more than he did the face. He held the picture closer, thought he could see something in the facial features.

"What was your father's mother's name?"

"Siggá."

Ánte jumped up from the couch. Áhkko looked at him, puzzled.

"I need to show you something," he said. "Wait. I'll be right back."

"Goodness, but you're in a hurry," she said. Her face wrinkled when she laughed.

He was already in the entryway and when he opened the front door, cold air rushed at him. He called out goodbye. His shoelaces slithered like long worms on the ground as he hurried home. He wished he could move faster but the soles of his boots refused to gain traction on the ice. The wind pushed him from behind and he slid along.

ÁNTE OPENED THE BOOK at Áhkko's kitchen table and turned to the right page. The light from the lamp framed the three people in the picture.

"Gehtja," he said.

She squinted. Put her finger on the photo and kept it there, as if searching for something. Her chair creaked when she leaned back and looked up at Ánte.

"Of course it's them," she said. "Muv áhkko ja áddjá. It looks like it was taken nearby?"

"I thought so too. Did they live here?"

"They were nomadic and moved with the reindeer. Just like my parents."

Áhkko looked more closely at the picture.

"They must have stopped by here sometime, in the fall."

"Did you know they were in this book?"

She shook her head.

"I've never seen this book."

"So Ánnda is my . . ."

"He was my grandfather," she said.

This information settled inside of him. He really was one of them—one of those people that he had not been able to see himself in. But they shared something. History, culture, blood.

Áhkko bent over the book again. Slowly turned the pages. It was difficult for her to separate the thin pages. She lifted a finger to her mouth and wet it with her tongue. When she read, she followed along with her fingertip right under the line, as if to remember where on the page she was.

"It's terrible that this research was allowed to go on for so long."

He didn't know what to say.

"And it's too bad that they told us so little," Áhkko continued. "My parents. As a child, you don't know to ask."

He looked at his grandmother sitting there next to him. The age spots. Her fingers. Her thin, light strands of hair. He was filled with a sudden sense of longing for her. He needed her, needed somebody to hold on to. A connection to history. Áhkko was the only one who could tell the story.

"I never really knew my mother," she said.

"Why not?"

"We were separated from our parents so early. Started nomad school and had to be boarded. We rarely saw them back then." She sighed. "And we weren't allowed to speak Sámi at school. The staff made sure we didn't. I think that's the easiest way to attack a people—you start with the children."

Ánte thought of Áhkko as a child. The little girl with the long braids. His heart ached for her.

"We are so lucky to have you young people today, so smart and competent. You won't let yourselves be defeated, that's for sure."

Áhkko put her hand on his head and pulled him closer. The chair legs lifted a little as he leaned toward her, letting her stroke his hair as if he were a young child. He pulled her warm scent into his lungs. It was painful when she touched his forehead; her dry skin scratched. But he didn't say anything. That was exactly how he wanted it to feel.

He closed his eyes. Imagined that he was still little and that Áhkko was holding him in her arms. Wished briefly that she would always hold him close like this.

She mumbled in his ear:

"They will never beat you."

"ARE YOU COMING to the party tomorrow, Ánte?"

He was staring out the window. Patches of dry ground had begun thawing out; wet grassy spots still covered with autumn leaves. But it would snow many times before spring. This time of year, the weather couldn't decide what to do. It took a long time for winter to let go.

"Hello?"

Máhttu shoved him. He startled.

"What?"

Juhán leaned across the table between them, drumming on the wood with his fingertips. It looked like he was playing the piano, but he didn't have piano fingers and the only sound resulting from his movement was a loud tapping.

"Come to the party," he said.

"What party?"

Máhttu laughed.

"Where are your ears?"

"You can't miss the night of your life," Juhán said.

Erik sat across from Ánte, hands folded on the table. He was wearing a bracelet around his wrist, a black leather band embroidered with a silvery pewter thread. It peeked out from under the edge of his sleeve.

"Maybe," Ánte said. "If I have time."

Juhán sighed loudly.

"How can you not have time on a Saturday?" He slammed his hand on the table so hard it shook. A few girls walked by, laughing. He raised his voice. "Why do you *never* want to party?"

Ánte shrugged.

"It would be nice if you came," Erik said, putting his hands in his lap.

Why did he say that? Ánte looked at Erik's thumbs rubbing against each other. Skin on skin. He would have liked to be there, right between them.

"What else are you going to do?" Máhttu asked, poking Ánte in the arm, hard.

Ánte moved away from him, leaned against the wall.

"I have a life, don't I?"

"A date with Yourown Hand, perhaps," Juhán said.

"How old are you?" said Erik. "Twelve?"

"Or he's planning a quiet evening at home. Watching a nice movie."

"Maybe a nice Disney movie with the family," said Máhttu.

"Oh hell," Juhán said. "I remember being in love with Jasmine from *Aladdin*. She was so fucking sexy."

"Ariel was much hotter."

"Shit, Máhttu, she has a fish butt. How would you fuck her?"

"Sounds like you watched these movies when you were a lot older than the intended audience," Erik said. "Or you were obsessed with sex when you were five."

Outside the window, snow had started to fall. It looked like white rain as it rushed to the ground. It looked like it would fall forever.

Ánte glanced at Erik. Would he bring Julia to the party? Maybe not, if they were thinking about breaking up.

Maybe they already had? After all, he had practically asked Ánte to come. Butterflies fluttered in Ánte's stomach.

"Erik was probably crushing on somebody like Ursula," Juhán said.

"Or that crippled old lady in Notre Dame," Máhttu said.

"That's a guy, you idiot. Erik's not fucking gay."

"For real? I thought it was a woman."

Juhán looked at Erik and Ánte to try to get them on his side.

"The hunchback of Notre Dame is a guy. Am I right?"

"Yes," Ánte said. "He falls in love with . . . with Esmeralda."

Erik laughed quietly. Ánte's face heated up, he looked down at the table. Words and pictures had been carved into the wood with keys and pencils.

"I knew you were watching Disney movies every weekend," Máhttu said.

Hearts, stick figures and sex organs. A swastika. *Philip loves Tova. Cock. Motherfucker. Queer.*

Fucking pansy.

"And he's still a thousand times more mature than you are," Erik said.

"Well, thank you."

Ánte yanked his phone from his pocket. Almost dropped it on the desk but caught it just in time. The screen felt sticky under his thumb.

"It's nine after," he said. "Class starts in a minute."

"Are you imagining Ella in one of those seashell bras that Ariel wears?" Juhán asked. "When you're alone in bed at night."

Máhttu's face changed colors. He moved his hand over his forehead, brushed a few stray hairs aside, laughed without smiling.

"Give it up already."

"A little sensitive?"

Ánte stood up from the bench, waited for Máhttu to move so he could get out. Máhttu looked at him.

"Where you going?" he asked.

"Class is starting. It already started, probably."

"What do we have?" Juhán asked. "I don't fucking know if I have it in me."

Ánte shoved Máhttu's legs aside and took a few steps away from the bench. Looked at his phone again. Then he hurried to the locker, grabbed his computer and started for the classroom.

He heard steps behind him, coming closer. He walked faster, had no energy left for Juhán and Máhttu. If he could only close his ears. He longed for silence. Just one more class, then he would go home. Only one class left.

Panting breaths behind him.

"You sure are running!"

He slowed down, allowed Erik to catch up.

"I just got tired of their talk."

"Yeah, I get that." Erik scratched his neck. "Feel like going to the party, then?"

"Maybe," Ánte said. He searched for something in Erik's eyes. An understanding. If Erik wanted him there, he'd obviously go, no matter how hard it was.

"We can go if you want," Erik said.

We. The two of them, together. No Julia. That must mean something. Ánte nodded. Smiled at the floor.

"I'll text you tomorrow," he said.

Juhán and Máhttu's voices could be heard from several meters behind them. They were slamming their lockers.

"We're out of here!" Juhán called through the hallway. "But you better fucking come to the party!"

HE WAS SLOUCHING on the couch, the controller in his lap. This was where he'd been most of Saturday, waiting for Erik to read his text. Ánte had asked when he wanted to head over to the party, but Erik had not responded yet.

The cushions had taken the shape of his body. When Erik wasn't around, Ánte could concentrate again. He was playing much better, slid past three defensive players and kicked the ball into the goal. Wished that the others could have seen him. Or just Erik. Maybe he would have been impressed, leaned back on the couch, smiled to himself. Glanced at Ánte, who would only have noticed by the tingling on his skin.

Ánte's mom came into the living room.

"Are you going to play all day? Your eyes will turn into squares."

He looked at the clock. Twenty to nine.

"The TV is not a square," he said. "It's a rectangle."

"I want to watch *Top Gun*. It's probably already started."

"I should have a TV in my room."

His mom sighed and sat down next to him. Put her hand under her chin and leaned on the armrest.

"What do you actually do in that game?"

"Play soccer," he said.

"Yeah, but what else?"

He finished the game. A picture of Alex Morgan appeared in the main menu. She was about to kick, her eyes glued on the ball in the frozen moment.

"Do you think she's cute?" his mom asked.

Ánte looked at her. She raised her eyebrows.

"But she is, isn't she?"

"You think that's what I care about."

"Ánte."

He picked up his phone from the table. Erik had still not replied. What if he wasn't going? Ánte sent a text to Ida, asked if she was going to the party. Maybe she could save him if Erik didn't show up. But when the phone buzzed he was disappointed.

Ida: *Am sick, but you WILL go!! Somebody needs to keep track of all the juicy stuff I'm missing.*

Ánte was not particularly interested in keeping track of anything juicy. Since when was that his job? She had friends there, didn't she? He started typing up a bunch of excuses but had not even sent them before Ida wrote again.

Ida: *I know what you're thinking.*

Ida: *DON'T object.*

That very moment Juhán sent three pictures on Snapchat, one right after the other: a blurred selfie, Máhttu doing a thumbs-up with a beer can in the other hand and a picture of three girls on the other side of the room, who clearly didn't know that their picture was being taken. It was obvious that Juhán had zoomed in on them: the picture was out of focus and their faces turned away.

"I'm leaving," Ánte said to his mom.

"Where are you going?"

"To Juhán's."

"Have you seen *Top Gun*? It's really good, actually. I remember when I was your age and—"

"I don't want to see some family movie."

She laughed.

"It's not a family movie. Tom Cruise is in it."

He stood up and placed the controller in the plastic box that his mom had put next to the TV bench. Juhán sent another snap. It was a clip of people dancing in the living room. He wrote: *But where is Ánte?*

Ánte played the video again, looked for Erik but didn't see him. He opened the chat and wrote.

Ánte: *Who's there?*

Juhán's picture appeared at the bottom frame. Ánte stared at it until the answer came.

Juhán: *Get over here and you'll see.*

Three emojis followed Juhán's text. They were winking.

THE FLOOR WAS VIBRATING from the bass when Ánte kicked his shoes off. He threw his coat in the pile on the floor. The music throbbed inside his rib cage, made his skeleton rattle with the beat.

A hard fist in his back.

"*Ánte,*" Juhán yelled. "You came!"

Juhán's face looked droopy, the corners of his mouth sagged. Like a rubber mask that was too big. His eyes were shiny as if he had a fever.

Ánte made a face from the loud noise. He had to yell to be heard over the music.

"Seriously, you're already drunk?"

"Nooo," Juhán said. His smile trickled out of the corners of his mouth.

Máhttu pushed his way in behind Juhán, patted Ánte on his shoulder. His hand was large and warm. Ánte could tell he was sweating even through the fabric of his shirt.

"Hey, Ánte."

Ánte smiled at Máhttu. Tried to see past the two of them into the living room. The room was full of bodies, some moving close to one another, others standing along the walls with beer cans in their hands. Heads bobbing and feet stomping to the music. Everybody in their whole community was probably here.

"Erik here yet?"

Juhán shook his head so hard his hair ended up in his eyes.

"He refuses," he said. "Was gonna hang with his chick."

Darkness inside. Ánte swallowed, tried to gain control over his stormy feelings. But it didn't work, it was too much—the only thing he could do was escape. He took one step back, out in the entryway, picked up a shoe from the floor. Dug around until he found the other one in the pile. Wobbled when he lifted his leg. Lost his balance.

"What are you doing?" Máhttu asked. "Where are you going?"

He could barely talk.

"Just forgot something."

Juhán put his hands on Ánte's shoulders, pulled him back and leaned his forehead against his. If Ánte had had antlers, he would have headbutted him.

"So fucking not, little Erik stalker. Hang out with us for once!"

Máhttu laughed and stumbled into the shoe pile. Juhán's hands were damp on Ánte's shoulders. Ánte clenched his teeth and dropped the shoe on the floor. Fought to disguise his feelings.

"There's lots of beer here," Juhán said in his ear. His breath was warm. "And girls. I'm gonna get Hanna later, you'll see."

His words were slurred, garbled, didn't quite reach all the way. Ánte couldn't have cared less about beer or girls right now. Máhttu grinned and shook his head. Ánte didn't know why.

"Mhm."

Juhán and Máhttu pulled him back into the sea of people.

The room was boiling. He pushed his way past sweaty bodies, reached a wall and leaned against it. Closed his eyes. It felt like his head were about to explode.

He could still see Juhán and Máhttu in the crowd, watched as they moved away. Juhán took a few unsteady dance steps. Máhttu shoved him toward the kitchen. They soon drowned in the crowd and could no longer be seen.

Every time somebody walked by, Ánte looked the other way. Down at the floor, to the other side of the room, up in the ceiling. Wished he were invisible. He took his phone from his pocket, pretended to focus on something. Pretended to be doing something very important so nobody would bother him. No messages from Erik. Nothing. He opened Instagram and scrolled through the feed without really looking.

Until he saw him.

The picture was dark, but he still recognized Erik's profile. The hair fading into the shadows, his eyes closed. His nose touching Julia's cheek. His lips touching her lips.

Half a year with you.

Erik was the one who had posted the picture. Julia had commented with a bunch of hearts in different colors and kissy-face emojis. Erik had replied with a single heart. A lot of people had said congratulations. That they were so sweet together, asked when they were getting married.

You are the cutest couple OMG.

Ánte wanted to throw his phone through the window. Break something. Scream. What the *hell* was Erik doing? You don't celebrate a six-month anniversary with somebody you're about to dump. Erik called Julia superficial, but he was the one who posted their kissy picture on Instagram. What a hypocrite.

Ánte touched the small blue rectangle that said *Following*, let his thumb hover over it. Would Erik notice? Maybe it would be too obvious and strange to unfollow him. Though would Erik even care? Probably not. He probably didn't care about Ánte at all.

He touched the rectangle to unfollow. The picture disappeared from the feed. A picture of a snowmobile popped up instead.

"Hi, Ánte!"

He slid the phone into his pocket. Hanna was standing in front of him. It took a while before he recognized her. Her lips were raspberry red, her eyes golden. Shiny. Her hair seemed even longer than the last time. It reached all the way to her waist.

"Hey," he said. Hesitantly.

"How are you?" she asked. "Or, I mean, how are things?"

He laughed, wondered what she would have said if he told her how things really were. He looked at the wallpaper pattern when he answered.

"Um, good."

Hanna nodded. Ánte looked down at his feet. One sock had gotten wet—a dark spot was spreading across the material—he didn't want to know how.

"Nice that you're here," she said. "Ida wasn't sure."

"What do you mean?"

"She didn't know if you'd be here. But she said she'd try to talk you into it."

Hanna snorted, made a strange gesture with her hand. Ánte raised his eyebrows and tried to smile but his mouth felt stiff. Why wasn't Hanna with Juhán? Maybe she was looking for him.

"Who are you with?" she asked.

"Juhán and Máhttu," he said, nodding toward the kitchen. "They're in there with the beer."

Hanna laughed and put her hand on his arm. He startled and she pulled her hand back as if she'd been burned.

"You don't like beer?"

"Not as much as they do."

She wound a strand of hair around her finger. Why didn't she leave?

"Me neither."

Ánte looked at Hanna. She was standing very close. She smelled faintly of sweat and some flowery perfume. Her eyelashes were so long that they grazed her cheeks when she blinked.

"My friends are in the kitchen too," she said. "The only thing they do is drink and make out with guys they don't even like. How fun is that? Too bad Ida is sick."

He nodded. Didn't know what else to do. Looked around for Juhán and Máhttu, but they were nowhere to be seen. Were they some of the guys that her friends didn't like? Wouldn't Juhán come and look for Hanna soon?

"Sounds boring."

"Uh-huh. But you don't have a girlfriend, do you?"

Ánte knit his eyebrows and became aware of his hands. He used one hand to comb through his hair.

"What?"

Her mouth trembled a little when she opened it.

"No, I mean, like . . ."

He shook his head. Put his hand in his pocket.

"No girlfriend."

She touched the pearl in her earlobe; the skin around it was red. Maybe she picked at it a lot. Her eyes swept over Ánte before she looked down on the floor. The pearl spun round and round. He wished she could make her stop.

"But hey, I was going to . . . ," he said.

Hanna sucked on her lower lip, like she was thinking about something. She looked up. Her face had changed color. When she opened her mouth, he saw that some of her lipstick had gotten stuck to her teeth.

"Won't you stay a little longer?" she asked. "I don't know who else to hang out with."

She looked so young standing there and a part of Ánte wanted to touch her cheek. He didn't know why.

"You could go to your girlfriends. Or to Juhán."

She frowned, shook her head, causing a strand of hair to fall down in front of her nose.

"Why would I go to Juhán?"

What did she mean? Was this not the same Hanna that Juhán had talked about? He had said that there was something going on between them. Had he meant somebody else? Maybe Ánte had misunderstood. When he thought about it, he realized that there must be at least one other Hanna in their school.

"I want to be with you," she continued, took a step closer, pulling the strand of hair behind her ear.

Her finger reached out and gently touched the back of Ánte's hand. He held his breath.

"What should we do?" she asked.

She leaned toward him and let the tip of her nose touch his. Stopped, hesitated. Her breath was soft and warm, smelled a little of mint. Ánte stood still, his body frozen. Hanna's lower lip grazed his.

And then she kissed him.

He didn't think it was supposed to feel like this. Their lips were stiff, their movements rigid and awkward. Their kisses were out of sync. He turned his head away, put his chin on her shoulder. Felt her thin lips against his neck.

Was this how Erik felt when he kissed Julia?

Ánte looked around the room. Everybody seemed to be watching him. He put a hand on Hanna's collarbone to push her away. She misunderstood his movement, grabbed his hand, squeezed it hard.

"What are you doing?" he asked. His voice was hoarse, cut its way through his throat.

She pulled back, a hint of confusion in her laughter.

"What? You don't want to?"

He didn't know what he wanted. It would have been so easy to just go along. Forget everything. Erik was with Julia right now anyway. Ánte didn't want to think about what they might be doing. It hurt much too much.

He pulled Hanna toward him, firmly. Didn't have it in him to care about Erik anymore. He brushed his finger along her bare arm, making the tiny hairs on her skin stand up.

Her hand on his jeans.

He couldn't meet her eyes. Instead, he let his hands explore her body. Touched the skin at her waist, moved his hand up under the edge of her shirt.

Now she kissed him more softly and he gave in. Tried to replace his thoughts of Erik with the picture of Hanna. Sank into the feeling. Her soft belly, the curve beneath her belly button. The little bump on her lower back, maybe it was a birthmark. Or a zit.

Her hands in the back pockets of his jeans. A warm finger inside the elastic of his underwear.

"Come on," she said. "Let's go."

He closed his eyes. The face between his hands was no longer Hanna's. It was Erik's nose that touched his. Erik's hair tickling his forehead. Erik's breath. Erik's lips.

"Hellooo," Hanna said. She grabbed his hand, tugged a little. "Are you coming?"

Her voice cut through the illusion; he broke away from her grip. Shook off the feeling.

She took a step back, searched his face.

"What is it?"

He shook his head. Shook and shook.

Hanna's lips were parted, as if she had not said everything she wanted to say. Her top had slid up by her waist. He wanted to reach out and pull it down, but then she would never let him go.

"I'm sorry," he said. "Sorry."

He turned his back to her, but she didn't say anything. Somebody dropped a glass when Ánte shoved by. A foaming puddle on the floor. He stepped over it, ignored the swearing behind him. Searched through the pile in the hallway, pulled his shoes on without tying them. He had to spread his toes to keep them on.

The night air grabbed him on the other side of the door, his shoes sank in the snow. Had he been wearing a coat? The wind seized him, pulled his hair, forced its way in under his clothes. He walked so fast it made him pant.

When he looked up, he saw it—the northern lights. They moved in waves across the sky, so forcefully that the stars had to get out of the way. Green flames danced in the dark, spread across the sky. It was happening. Right now. The end of the world.

The hunter had shot. And missed.

HIS LUNCH SAT uneaten on the plate. Ánte picked at his rice, made patterns with his fork. Put his silverware down when he noticed that Erik's eyes were stuck on his hands.

"I was so unbelievably hungover yesterday," Juhán said. "Slept till like four."

Máhttu nodded and yawned so they could see the entire inside of his mouth.

"I still feel dead. We should have Mondays off too."

Erik laughed. The light from the cafeteria windows lit up his eyes. He still had not said anything about why he didn't get in touch on Saturday. Maybe he'd even forgotten. It probably didn't even mean anything to him.

Ánte was quiet, wondered how to change the topic. He felt Juhán's eyes on him. Lifted his glass of water. Took a gulp. His mouth turned cold.

"I heard something," Juhán said. He reached across the table and touched Ánte's shoulder with the back of his knife. "That Ánte scored at the party. Got laid?"

Ánte coughed, making water spray out all over his plate. Kernels of rice floated around in the liquid. Máhttu backed away from him, a disgusted look on his face. Ánte glanced at Erik but saw no reaction on his face. How could he be so indifferent?

"Of course not."

Juhán looked at Máhttu and Erik as if Ánte were totally crazy.

"Seriously? You could have gotten laid for the first time and you blew it."

"I didn't blow it."

"Who was it? You left before we even had a chance to talk to you."

Ánte threw his napkin on his plate, leaned back in his chair. He could feel his heartbeat on the back of his chair. Had not noticed how hard the chair was until now.

"Her name is Hanna."

Still no reaction from Erik. Only Juhán. He dropped his silverware on the table, causing them to clatter against one other.

"*Hanna* Hanna?"

Ánte shook his head.

"Not your Hanna. I asked, but she didn't seem to understand what I meant when I mentioned you."

Erik looked at his plate. Cut the grouse into minuscule chunks. Ánte looked at the pewter bracelet on his wrist. Julia probably had one just like it. *A perfect couple,* everybody had written. Traitor. There was obviously nothing Ánte could say that would make Erik care.

"Are you serious?" Juhán said. "There was only one Hanna at the party."

Ánte understood absolutely nothing. Had she lied to him? Or was Juhán lying?

How could you have *something going on* without her knowing?

Juhán looked away. His jaw tensed.

"Whatever. You knew I liked her."

"Seriously," Ánte said. "I didn't do anything, not really. She was the one who kissed me."

Máhttu raised his hands.

"Come on, guys. Bros before hos?"

"What the hell," Juhán said. His face had turned dark. "I didn't even think you liked girls, Ánte."

It turned quiet. Ánte couldn't breathe. His windpipe was as narrow as a straw. He could feel his heart ticking through it.

"What did you say?"

"I don't know, you've never seemed that interested." Juhán shrugged. "Maybe you're gay."

For the first time, Erik raised his eyes to look at Ánte. They were all quiet.

"I lied," Ánte said finally. He didn't look at Erik.

"About what?" Juhán leaned back in his chair. He looked like he was about to grin.

Ánte could hear his own blood coursing through him. He could feel it all the way out in his fingertips.

"About me and Hanna." He put his hands in his lap, didn't want anybody to see them shaking. "We did have sex. I just didn't want you to get mad."

Juhán's face emptied—his feelings seemed to have seeped out of him, onto the floor. Erik was still staring at Ánte. Máhttu too. The entire cafeteria was probably staring. He didn't dare look around to see if it was true.

He stood up, accidentally shoving Máhttu with his elbow. Máhttu didn't say anything. The plate felt slippery in Ánte's grip. The silverware slid around on top.

He hesitated, opened his mouth. Closed it. Opened it.

"And Máhttu," he said. "She's not a *ho*."

Outside the cafeteria, he realized he was shaking. He jogged all the way back to the school building even though his lungs were protesting. Hurried to his locker. It took too long to unlock it. It refused to cooperate. The lock rattled and rattled until it finally fell open.

He threw his coat on, pulled his hat too far down his forehead, slammed the locker shut. He stared at the floor until he was out of the building.

He didn't know when the next bus was leaving, didn't even know what time it was. He picked up his phone to find the bus schedule. It was difficult to type with cold fingers.

A movement out of the corner of his eye made him turn around.

Somebody in a black down jacket had come out the door behind him, wide heels sinking through layers of fresh snow. A bag over one shoulder. The blonde hair, reaching to her waist, danced in the wind when she ran.

"ÁNTE, WAIT!"

Hanna caught up with him, panting. She rearranged her hair, moved her bangs behind her ear and moved her bag higher up on her shoulder. She was not wearing pearls in her earlobes today.

"What do you want? I have to get on the bus."

"Skipping?"

"Are you?" He nodded at her bag.

She picked at her zipper.

"I was on my way to lunch, but when I saw you rushing out I figured you weren't coming back. I have something to tell you."

He scraped the ground with one foot. Looked for an escape route. The yard in front of the school was too small. There was nowhere to go. There was no way she could have heard what he said already, was there? She hadn't even been in same building when it happened. But maybe Juhán had texted her or even called.

What if she knew?

"The teacher was sick."

"Sure." She gave him a lopsided smile. "Where are you going?"

"Home," he said. What if somebody saw him through the windows? And with Hanna, of all people. He started walking backward. "Have you talked to Juhán?"

"What?"

Hanna followed him. She was steadier on her feet, even though she was wearing heels.

"I just wanted to say I'm sorry," she said.

"What do you mean? I'm the one who left."

Hanna tipped her head. She looked soft today, softer than on Saturday. Ánte felt lighter, let the air out. She must not have heard.

"I don't know," she said. "Everything just turned out so wrong."

"Like you just happened to kiss the wrong guy, or what?"

"Oh, cut it out!" she moaned. "Is it so hard to understand that *you're* the one I want to kiss?"

Ánte couldn't help smiling at her words. Hanna laughed when she saw it. Her lips were light. Maybe she wasn't wearing makeup.

She wiped the corner of her eye.

"When did you say the bus was leaving?"

"Don't know," he confessed. "I didn't have time to check before you interrupted me."

"You're such a liar," she laughed.

The nausea returned. He tried to push it away, focused on the trees by the side of the road. Their branches were moving carefully in the wind.

"You know what I think?" she said.

"What?"

"I think you actually like me."

The corners of his mouth were as heavy as rocks when Ánte tried to smile. He backed up, fixed his hat, moved his bangs from his forehead.

A white bus with red and blue stripes came driving along the road.

"There it is," he said, nodding at the bus. "Gotta go."

Hanna smiled a little and nodded. Looked down on the ground, then up again.

The wind made her eyes shiny. There was something about her eyes. Now it felt almost sad to leave her.

The thought made him hesitate. If he could only have liked Hanna for real, things would have been so easy. She seemed to like him, and Erik had Julia, after all. They would probably never break up.

He inhaled.

"Coming?"

"What?" She raised her eyebrows. "To your place?"

"Or we can go to yours. Wherever you live."

Hanna looked happy.

"Then we don't have to take the bus," she said. "Come on!"

THEIR STEPS ECHOED in the stairway. Hanna unlocked the door and let Ánte enter first.

"You live alone?" he asked.

"No," she said, kicking her shoes off in the entryway. "My mom's at work."

He had already forgotten that it was just past lunch and that they were both skipping school. He felt bad suddenly. He hardly knew himself.

Was he supposed to hang his coat on a hanger or on the hooks? he wondered. And where was he supposed to put his shoes and then what was he supposed to do or say? Hanna leaned against the wall and looked at him. She twisted a strand of hair around her finger. He wondered what she expected, wondered what he himself had been thinking.

"Do you . . . um, want something to drink?"

He shrugged.

"Not really."

They stood there, quiet. Ánte put his hands in his pockets. Looked around the entryway. Looked at the hat shelf, the picture on the wall, the shoes. Hanna was biting her lip.

"Let's do something fun," she said. "Now that we're skipping anyway."

"Like what?"

"Like, make out."

He stiffened and she giggled.

"I was *joking*! Relax, you don't have to be so scared all the time!"

"Who knows, I might end up kissing the wrong guy by mistake."

Hanna's laughter stopped, her face crumpled. Ánte's blood coursed through his body. Didn't she get that he was using the same joke as at the bus stop?

"What do you mean, 'guy'?" She picked at her earlobe even though there was nothing there. "Are you, like, gay?"

Ánte laughed, but it felt forced. There was something wrong with his throat.

"I was *kidding*," he said. Tried to imitate her tone of voice.

But Hanna looked skeptical. Now what should he do? He took a few steps closer to her. Didn't know where he got the courage. Maybe it was panic, fear, adrenaline.

"How about this?" he said and pushed her against the wall, put his hands on her cheeks. They were warm beneath the palms of his hands.

Hanna's eyes got bigger. They closed just as he kissed her.

Her lips were as hot as fire. Softer this time. Welcoming. Her hands around his head. A few fingers crept up along his neck, caressed his hair above his ear.

"Now do you believe me?" he whispered into her lips.

Hanna nodded, her forehead against his. It felt as if his ribs might break. As if his entire skeleton might fall apart.

She giggled.

"Why are you laughing?"

Her arms around him, she put her cheek against his.

"It's just that you make me happy."

He hugged her back. Put his nose between her neck and her shoulder, inhaled her smell. For some reason this made him teary. He closed his eyes.

"Want me to be honest?" she asked right by his ear.

"Of course."

"Promise not to think I'm strange."

He nodded, his face still on her neck. It felt safer to not have to look her in the eye.

"I've thought about you for a really long time, long before the party. I just didn't have the courage to say anything. Or do anything. Ida tried to help me, but I just . . ."

Ánte's phone buzzed in his jean pocket.

"God, I shouldn't have told you that. Sorry. I'm just so happy to finally be with you, I thought I didn't have a chance after what happened. But now you're here."

His phone buzzed again. Hanna seemed confused, looked down.

Ánte backed up a few steps and retrieved his phone. He didn't know what else to do.

"Just need to see if it's important."

Ida: *Heard you and Hanna made out at the party????*

Ida: *Impressive*

Ida: *Though a little unexpected*

Ida: *I had the impression you weren't interested*

Ida: *Why do all interesting things happen when I'm sick?*

He locked his screen but kept his phone in his hand. Ida was right. What was he doing? Here he was, at the house of a girl he had made out with—not just once, but twice—while skipping school after having an argument with his friends. He was here, even though every part of his body wished he was somewhere else. He regretted having come with her, wished he had just gotten on the bus and gone home.

"Who was that?" Hanna crossed her arms over her chest.

"My dad. I guess he knows I'm skipping," Ánte said. He stared at the pattern of the rug in the hallway. "I have to go."

"Okay, but you'll be in touch later?"

He nodded. Put his coat on as fast as he could. Lifted his hand to wave before closing the door behind him. It slammed shut louder than he had meant it to.

WATER WAS DRIPPING from the rooftops. The roads had begun to thaw, leaving bare spots covered in sand and gravel. There was still snow, but Ánte saw through the window that the piles were softening, shrinking.

He was on the couch looking out, his mom knitting at the other end.

"Hey," she said. "I heard something."

He was tired of people hearing things.

"Okay?"

"Did you meet somebody?"

"Meet who?"

"Hanna, is that her name? Isn't her mom the one who works at the city hall?"

"But how the f—" He stopped himself, gave up. This was insane.

"I'm your mom," she said. "Moms want to know everything."

"I really don't think you do."

She let her knitting sink down in her lap, raised her eyebrows over her reading glasses. She pulled at the dark blue skein, fiddled with the yarn.

"Ida is the one who mentioned it. Are you going out?"

He leaned against the windowpane, watched the drops. How they fell. What had he gotten himself into? Soon he would no longer be able to get out. Maybe it was best to just go along.

"I can tell something's going on."

"What?"

"You seem different. Are you in love?"

He refrained from saying the words at the tip of his tongue. Focused on the soft snowdrifts. They sparkled in the sun. The tips of the fir trees were yellow. As if they had been dipped in light.

"I need to get out on the snowmobile sometime," he said. "Before all the snow is gone."

His mom smiled and shook her head.

"You're good at changing the subject."

She put her knitting down and turned to Ánte. Put her hand on his shoulder.

"Call Hanna," she said.

"We don't call each other," he said.

"Then write. On Snapchat or whatever it's called."

"We don't usually write on Snapchat."

She smiled.

"Ánte."

He turned around on the couch and she lifted his feet into her lap. He put them down again. She sighed. Pulled him toward her and put her face in his hair. She was warm, smelled like coconut lotion.

"My little boy is growing up," she said. "My tiny little boy."

His eyes were closed, he focused on his mother's smell. Felt her breathing on his scalp. Her voice warmed his head.

"Whoever your first girlfriend will be, she's the luckiest girl in the world."

He couldn't help wondering what she would have said if she knew the truth. Would she have been this happy if he went out with Erik?

She put her arm around him. He hid his face against her shoulder. Something was happening to his lips, something he couldn't control. He wiped a tiny drop from the corner of his eye.

ÁNTE WALKED BACK and forth in his room, thought of kicking the wall but stopped himself. He didn't want his parents to hear it. The feeling created tension in every part of his body. He regretted everything he had ever done. Everything was ruined. Exactly everything. Why couldn't he just be like everybody else?

It was too late now. The sky had already been set on fire.

He picked up his phone and went to Erik's Instagram. Looked at the picture. *Half a year with you.* Why did he write like that, as if it were only for Julia? He had tagged Julia in the picture. In her feed were even more pictures of the two of them together.

Erik and Julia close together in a speedboat. Blue mountains and dark water all around them.

Erik and Julia in the restaurant goahte at the market.

Julia wearing Erik's shirt, too big and open in the neck.

Erik sleeping, hair disheveled and eyes closed. His face looked so soft. Beautiful.

Ánte picked up his pillow from his bed and smashed it. Tore down the plastic plant that his mom had put on the dresser when the real one died. The pot fell on the floor. He saw that the top dresser drawer was open. Inside he glimpsed the book.

He yanked the drawer open. The book was beige now. It no longer had a name. First he threw it on the floor. It landed next to the plastic plant, stared up at him. He sat down on the floor and opened it. Started tearing out all the pages with photos on them, one by one. Curled his fingers angrily around them. Tore. Ripped. A photo of a woman in profile flew up in the air, floated back down. She wasn't wearing any clothes.

He picked up the photo, squeezed it into a little ball. How small did the pieces have to be before there was nothing left? How much more tearing would he have to do?

He found the page with Ánnda and Siggá's picture. Took out a pair of scissors and cut along the edges. He cut out Harald Lundgren, crushed him with his fist. That's how easy it was to destroy.

Then he took the separate pieces of the cut-up photo and taped the couple together next to each other.

The air went out of him. He looked at the shreds of paper around him, at the picture of his grandmother's grandparents. It was painful to see them. He accidentally folded a corner of the photo when he put it back in the book. Did it even mean anything that they were related if he couldn't be like them? Maybe they wouldn't even have liked him. Not if they had known who he really was.

If he didn't get his act together soon, nobody would like him anymore.

When he went on Facebook he realized that he didn't know Hanna's last name. After looking through Ida's friends list he found her and sent her a friend request. Before she could accept it, he messaged her.

Ánte: *You were right in what you said.*

It didn't take long for her to write back.

Hanna: *What?*

Ánte: *That I like you.*

This time her answer took a little longer. The bubbles next to Hanna's profile picture disappeared, then reappeared.

Hanna: *Like, for real?*

Ánte: *Yeah, for real.*

Hanna: *I guess it's pretty obvious, but I like you too.* ❤

ANTE SAT ALONE on the bus to school. The other guys wouldn't even look at him. Not that he wanted to be with them either. Especially not Erik. His whole body objected.

He couldn't focus during the first period. Pushed his pencil so hard against the paper that the graphite pulverized. Why would he care about the square root of *x* when everything was ruined? Solving an equation in his math book would solve nothing in the real world.

He held his head so still that his neck started to hurt. He refused to turn, in case he'd accidentally look at Erik or the others. When class was over, he was the first one out the door.

In the hallway outside he saw Hanna. She had sent a bunch of messages since yesterday. Embellished her words with hearts and flowers. Texting with her was much more entertaining than he had thought. She was actually both fun and nice—and sometimes she made him forget his anxiety for a while. Everything could be so easy with Hanna if he would just make a small effort.

She waved and set course toward him.

"Hey, sweetie!"

She came so close that he automatically backed up. His back hit the locker door. When he noticed Erik looking at him, he tried to get his act together. Reached out and rubbed Hanna's shoulder.

She smiled.

"What class do you have next?"

"Sámi," he said. "But not for another half hour."

Hanna moved her hand through his bangs, like he himself did sometimes. But the movement felt clumsy, his hair fell back in his face again.

She leaned closer, whispered. Her breath was warm on his ear.

"Why is Erik staring at us?"

Ánte didn't answer. Instead, he put his hand around her neck and pulled her even closer. Put his lips on hers. She seemed unprepared, but her lips quickly softened and she kissed him back.

A locker door slammed into his upper arm. Hanna jumped back.

"You're in my way," Erik said.

"Oh, sorry," she said. "Didn't know your locker was there."

Ánte didn't move a millimeter. Erik pushed the locker door so hard against him that it hurt. When he showed no reaction, Erik put a hand on his shoulder and shoved.

Ánte's body didn't care that he was furious; Erik's hand made everything inside him soften. He took a few unsteady steps to the side.

Hanna stared at him, eyes wide open. He just shook his head.

"Okay, I'll leave then," she said, but it sounded more like a question than a statement. "See you later."

Erik put his stuff in the locker and slammed it so hard that the sound cut through Ánte's ears. He fumbled with the padlock, swore under his breath when he couldn't get it to work. Then he turned to Ánte. His eyes made Ánte want to sink through the floor.

"What are you doing?"

Now that Hanna was gone, Ánte had nothing to defend himself with, no shield, nobody to hide behind. He crossed his arms over his chest to protect everything inside.

“I could ask you the same thing.”

“What does that mean?”

Ánte tensed his body to stop it from shaking.

“You never answered when I wrote. We were going to Juhán’s together.”

Erik sighed.

“It turned out to be our half anniversary. I didn’t know.”

Ánte looked down at his feet, scraped the floor with his shoe.

“Who the hell celebrates a half anniversary?”

“That’s exactly what I’ve been saying,” said Erik. “Those things are important to her. Or that other people know.”

“But *you* were the one who posted it on Instagram.”

“It’s not like it was my idea! And you don’t seem to have had that bad a time at the party, after all.”

Ánte didn’t know what to say. Erik leaned against the locker. He crossed his arms too.

“Why do you care so much about me and Julia? You have your own girlfriend now, don’t you.”

“Why do you care if I have a girlfriend?”

Erik smiled and shook his head. He looked like he was talking to a kid who didn’t understand anything.

“I couldn’t care less.”

Ánte’s nails cut into the palm of his hand.

“Well, good.”

Somebody cleared their throat behind him.

“Um, guys.”

Only now did Ánte notice Juhán and Máhttu standing off to the side, holding their books. They looked like they had seen a ghost.

Everybody just stood there, looking at anything but one other. The silence was unbearable until Ánte's pocket buzzed. He picked up his phone.

Hanna: *Ánte*

Hanna: *I need to talk to you*

Hanna: *Now*

HE COULD TELL right away that she had heard the rumor. Her eyes bored into him before she turned around and started walking toward a desk at the back of the hallway where it was quiet and empty. He followed behind her uncertainly. His pulse thought he was moving much faster than he was.

Hanna sat down on one side of the desk. Ánte sat across from her, picked at a hangnail on his thumb.

"Ella told me something. But I wanted to ask you first."

He tried to meet her gaze, but everything in him rebelled.

Hanna's mouth opened, but it took a while before any words came out.

"Is it true?" she began. "Did you say . . ."

"I know what you mean."

"I just don't understand . . . Why did you say that? I didn't even know if you wanted to . . ."

An eyelash had ended up by the corner of her eye. He didn't dare lean over and brush it away.

She made fists with her hands on the table in front of her.

"I just don't understand why you said that."

Ánte thought she would look down in her lap but she didn't. She looked right at him.

"I don't know. I'm sorry."

"Is that all you want from me? Sex?"

"No," he said. "No, absolutely not."

She pulled back.

"You absolutely *don't* want to have sex with me?"

"Yes, well, I suppose I do, but . . ."

"You wouldn't be weird if you did."

Ánte didn't answer, avoided meeting her eyes. Wished he could hide from them. When he didn't say anything, she laughed. Short and abrupt.

"You just don't like me, or what?"

He rubbed his face with his hands.

"It doesn't have to do with you. Not really."

"How can it not have to do with me?" Something shifted in her eyes. "You mean . . ."

She sighed. Shook her head.

"Oh god, but I'm stupid."

"What, why?"

"You've been using me all this time."

Not until then did she look out in the hallway. Her lips trembled a little. The eyelash had wandered down to her cheekbone. It would be so easy to blow it off.

He reached toward her.

"Hanna."

"Ánte," she said. "I don't want to talk to you anymore."

His hand fell to his thigh.

"That's okay."

Who was supposed to stay and who was supposed to leave? Was he being dumped, or was she?

"Know what?" She stood up. "I'm not the one who's stupid, you are. You're not fooling anybody going on like this."

He didn't want to be with Hanna. And yet, when she took her coat and left, something broke.

YOU'RE NOT FOOLING *anybody going on like this.* Her words played on repeat in his head, wouldn't stop. Hanna's voice, her steps when she walked away. If there had only been a button to push when you'd had enough. When all you wanted was silence. Forced stop. Start over.

He went on Hanna's Facebook page. Pushed the Message button.

Ánte: *What did you mean by what you said?*

The moment he clicked Send, he regretted it. She probably wouldn't even reply. But soon he saw her profile picture in the bottom corner.

Hanna: *That I don't want to talk to you anymore. Was that not totally clear? It goes for Messenger too, fyi.*

Ánte: *Not that, the part about me not fooling anybody.*

Hanna: *?*

Ánte: *Fooling who about what?*

Hanna: *What do you want?*

Ánte: *Just want to know.*

Hanna: *You have made me so incredibly sad, don't you get that?*

Hanna: *Don't write to me again.*

His phone ended up on the floor with a loud bang. It still didn't break. It didn't even get a scratch. He almost wished it had, that the screen had broken. A fractured pattern across the glass. He wanted something to feel more broken than him. But the screen just looked back at him, blank and unbroken. Hanna's words so much more self-assured than his.

THE SMELL OF NEWLY boiled potatoes filled the room when his mom put the pot on the table. She took a piece of Arctic char from the frying pan and put it on Ánte's plate.

"Are you going with your dad and Per-Ailo this weekend to check on the reindeer? They're about to calve."

"Is Erik going?" He wasn't sure what answer he wanted.

His mom shrugged and put fish on her own plate.

"Maybe."

His dad helped himself to a mountain of potatoes. There was barely enough room left for the rest of the food.

"You spend a lot of time with Erik these days," he said.

"We're friends."

If they still were.

His dad looked at him with knit eyebrows. Replied with his mouth full of potatoes; you could see the yellow mush when he chewed.

"Yeah, I know."

Ánte squirmed in his chair, deboned his fish as quickly as he could. Poured salt on the pink meat.

"He's with Hanna too," his mom said. "Isn't that nice?"

She put a hand on his dad's arm, but he moved away.

Ánte stuffed the char in his mouth, then the potatoes, peel on.

"Thanks for supper," he said.

"You're not done already, are you?"

He nodded, stood up, rinsed his plate but didn't put it in the dishwasher. The fish bones were sliding around on the plate. His mom's eyes followed him out of the kitchen.

He sat down at his desk with his computer. He had to finish reading what he hadn't read when he last visited the page, needed to know what it said. His fingers flew across the keys.

Homosexual reindeer herders.

In the search results he found the link he had clicked on earlier. The forum slogan lit up in blue behind the name: *True Freedom of Speech.*

The person who had started the discussion thread asked if homosexual Sámis existed. He talked about his own experience working in Kiruna. He had met reindeer herders there who had not been very accepting of it. They had not seemed very interested in sex at all, he believed. Maybe they didn't have it in their genes. Did anybody know?

None of the people who replied seemed to be Sámi. A guy from Gothenburg mentioned that he had met a homosexual Sámi in a bar in the city. Ánte stored away every word in his memory bank.

TheFox91: *The gay Lapp you claim to know is hardly a reindeer herder, just a wannabe. I have never personally heard of a homosexual Sámi.*

His stomach tightened. Without stalling too long in one place, he kept scrolling.

DrHazz: *Theoretically, there should be homosexual reindeer herders.*

TheFox91: *Hardly, not anymore. Most likely, they all killed themselves :)*

Ánte closed his computer and left it where it was. Walked out into the entryway and put his clothes on.

"Where are you going?" His mom stood in the doorway to the kitchen, drying a frying pan with a towel decorated with embroidered reindeer. They stared at him from the fabric.

"Out for a while."

She nodded.

Outside, he climbed on to his snowmobile. The sun had left pink traces across the sky. The snowmobile started with a rumble, emitting a soothing smell of gasoline. The trees watched quietly as he drove into the woods.

This time of year, the snow was soft and wet. If you took a step in the wrong direction, where it was still deep, it could swallow you whole. As when Ánte was playing in the snow once when he was four and his dad had to pull him out of a snowy grave. His boot had gotten stuck at the bottom and didn't find its way home until June.

The snowmobile bumped along the trail, screamed when he pressed the pedal down harder than the engine wanted to go. Conditions were not in his favor. He stopped the snowmobile and climbed off near a big tree. Kicked the trunk until his toes hurt.

"You're sick," he said. "So fucking sick."

He kicked and kicked until he was exhausted. Then he sank down, crouched, leaned his forehead against the trunk. Counted his breaths. Breathed in, breathed out.

His snow pants were getting wet. Ánte felt like a little kid, stuck deep in the snow again, unable to get out, waiting for his dad to come and get him, hold him in his arms, brush the snow from his pants. Hold him as closely as he only did back then.

No dad arrived.

Darkness crept closer, put its arms around him.

He climbed up on to the snowmobile, sat staring for a while before he turned the headlights on to light up the trail. Then he drove so fast that the trees had to move over; they took a step aside, let him pass. But the trees were not afraid of him. They had stood here for a very long time, he knew that—longer than he could imagine. Their roots stuck forever in the same soil.

HE OPENED THE CHAT.

Ánte: *What did you mean?*

Ánte: *Please*

Ánte: *Just answer*

Ánte: *I'm not trying to trick anyone*

Ánte: *Really need to know*

Ánte: *What did you mean?*

THE GUYS WERE STILL not talking to Ánte. When he sat down in their usual spot in the cafeteria, Juhán, Máhttu and Erik walked past him and sat several tables away. The chairs scraped as usual, but they weren't the right chairs. There was the usual clatter when they put their plates, silverware and glasses on the table, but it wasn't the right table.

Ánte squeezed his silverware in his hands until they were warm. He'd been sitting alone in the cafeteria for several days, wondered what people were thinking. He looked down at his plate while he ate.

A voice made him look up. Ida. Her friends had already moved on.

"Why are you sitting here?" she asked.

It was strange to see her. They had not seen each other since before the party, before she got sick.

"Are you feeling better?"

"Don't think you can change the subject that easily!"

He looked around. A few tables away, Hanna was pulling out a chair.

"We always sit here," he said. "Or, I do, I mean."

Ida knit her eyebrows and turned to look at the table where Juhán, Erik and Máhttu were sitting. The movement made her hair swing from side to side.

"Are you mad at them, or something?"

"Uh-huh," he said. "But mostly the other way around."

Ida's face creased with laughter. Ánte couldn't see what was so funny.

"Just go over there. They can't very well pull the chair out from under you."

Then she left, walked past the guys' table and continued on to her friends. The fabric in her wide pants flapped.

Ida's comment made everything even more embarrassing. Ánte took his silverware and plate in one hand, glass in the other. Stood up. An anxious ripple on the surface of the milk made it almost spill. None of the guys were looking in his direction as he moved closer.

The seat next to Erik was not available; Máhttu was sitting there. The only free chair was the one next to Juhán.

When Ánte put his stuff down, a drop of milk splashed on the table. Juhán let go of his silverware and picked up his phone.

"What the hell," he said, slapping the palm of his hand on the table. Another splash of milk on the table. "Fucking shit Jörgen."

"What?" Erik said.

"Got your grades?" Máhttu asked.

"What?" Ánte said.

Juhán scrolled on his phone, cleared his throat and read.

"So this is what he writes: *You have not used correct references.* What the hell even are references?"

"You talking about Swedish class?"

Juhán continued: "*I must ask you to revise your essay and turn it in again. Don't forget to add your sources at the end of the document.*"

Juhán looked up and smiled sarcastically at Erik and Máhttu. "Nice, eh?"

Erik shook his head.

"Did you even read what we were supposed to do?"

"Fuck Jörgen."

"It's not true," Ánte said.

"I'm getting fucking nervous now," Máhttu said. "I don't think I used references either."

"I didn't sleep with Hanna. It's not true."

Nobody said anything. Erik looked at his plate. Something was happening to the corners of his mouth. Ánte wanted to lean closer to see what was going on.

"Okay," Juhán said, and looked away. His jaw clenched. "But you obviously made out with her."

"It doesn't matter," Ánte said. "She's not even talking to me anymore."

Juhán looked up at the ceiling. His mouth was frozen.

Máhttu was looking at Ánte and Erik and you could feel through the table how his leg was bouncing up and down below it.

"Are you going to come back tomorrow and say you lied again?" Juhán asked.

"What?"

"I *absolutely did not* sleep with her, or yes, I did, no wait, I didn't." Juhán looked right at Ánte now. His eyes were as hard as glass. "Are you done?"

Máhttu's shoes were pounding holes in the floor.

Ánte nodded. He wondered what Erik was thinking. Didn't dare look at him. He had said he didn't care, but Ánte hoped it wasn't true. That nothing they had said that time was true.

Nobody was eating at their table. Maybe they had all finished. Ánte's stomach balked when he looked at the wild meat stew. A warm feeling rose behind his eyelids.

"I'm sorry," he said. "I didn't mean to hurt her. Or all of you. I'm sorry."

"Okay, okay," Juhán said. "Please don't start crying."

Ánte shook his head.

"I'm not going to."

Juhán turned to Ánte and looked at him for a while. His lips twitched. Then he gave him a light shove in the shoulder.

"Fine," he said.

HE KNEW ERIK was near him long before he saw him. A vibration in the air. Soon he heard his voice behind him in the hallway.

"Hey, you."

Erik grabbed Ánte's lower arm. The touch sent shivers through his body. Erik's cheeks were red, strands of hair had gotten tangled across his forehead. He lowered his voice.

"Hey, you," he said again. He still didn't let go. "I'm sorry."

"For what?"

"For not being in touch before the party. And for everything else."

Ánte looked at the fingers that encircled his wrist. Why was Erik holding on to him for so long? They had already stopped walking.

"You don't have to say you're sorry."

"Yes. You did. So I thought it was my turn."

Ánte shrugged. The movement made Erik let go.

"It's over with Hanna," he said. "Just so you know."

He wondered if it was over between Erik and Julia too, but didn't know how to ask.

Erik looked away, but before he did, Ánte caught a tiny smile. Was Erik happy about that? He had said he didn't care. But maybe he was thinking about something else.

"All right then," Erik said. He scratched the back of his neck. "Good to know."

They started walking side by side to the classroom. Once in a while, Erik smiled, as if he was thinking about something funny.

"What are you thinking about?"

Erik shook his head.

"Nothing."

"Tell me."

Their eyes met. A fire in Erik's eyes.

"I'm just happy."

Ánte looked at the floor again. That was almost exactly what Hanna had said when they kissed that second time. Though Erik clearly didn't mean what Hanna had meant. The words still made him warm.

"By the way," Erik said. "Are you going to come check on the reindeer this weekend?"

Ánte nodded.

"Are you?"

"I'm in," Erik replied, smiling.

THE REMAINING SNOW COVER was baking in the sun, enjoying its last moments on earth. Warm winds were blowing, causing the melting water from the snowdrifts high up to run down the moss-covered slopes.

It was spring in the mountains.

Erik's lips had taken on a soft tint of orange when he put down his coffee gukse. Warm orange. He was tapping his foot up and down, staring into the embers. The fire was about to go out.

Ánte's dad and Per-Ailo stood farther away. They were checking on the reindeer that were spread out over the bare spots on the ground. During calving season, the reindeer were more skittish than at other times—so it was important to keep your distance and let the females give birth in peace. But it was also important to look for predators and make sure nothing bad happened.

Ánte thought about saying something, but his voice had been locked away at the bottom of his stomach. Instead he pulled the visor of his cap down and closed his eyes.

Erik was the first to speak.

"Hey?"

"Yes?"

"I've talked to Julia now."

Ánte wasn't sure what he meant. He remembered the last time Erik had said something about Julia. What was he supposed to think?

But even though he didn't know, something started kicking around in his stomach. That stubborn hope.

"Okay?"

Erik sliced off a piece of coffee cheese, made it disappear in his gukse.

"I don't think she wants to live the life I live."

"What do you mean?"

"This." Erik motioned with his hand to indicate the reindeer and the Arctic tundra.

"Our life."

Did he mean it was over between him and Julia? Ánte didn't dare ask. He lay down on the reindeer pelt, dug his fingertips into the fur. Closed his eyes. Did his breathing always sound this strange? Was Erik wondering about it? Maybe he was thinking about it right now.

Erik bumped his upper arm. Ánte dragged himself up, wiped a hand across his face.

"What is it?"

He noticed Per-Ailo waving from a distance. Erik nodded at him.

"We'd better go now if we want to see any calves."

They stood up and carefully stepped closer. One of the females was about to give birth on a bare spot farther off. It was the white reindeer, Ánte's white reindeer that had been with his family for feeding in the winter. The little calf came out, wet, fur sticky. The female licked the calf and tried to help it off the ground. So small and fragile.

After a while it tried to stand up on skinny stick legs. They looked too long compared with the body, as if somebody had built the calf from twigs. It could barely get up—when it tried to take a step forward it fell.

Once again, the calf stood up. It stood still for a while, as if to feel the earth before it stumbled ahead. It took its first steps on wobbly legs.

Ánte closed his eyes. Relief washed over him like a wave. He had not expected it, was unprepared. The sun burned through his eyelids, everything turned red. And now, now, he could hear the willow grouse play.

Erik's bare hand touched Ánte's. He didn't open his eyes. Didn't want to open them now.

"How are you?" Erik's shoes squeaked on the snow. Maybe he was shifting his weight to the other leg.

Ánte listened to every sound that Erik's body made. Listened as carefully as he could.

"She'll make it," Erik continued. "It will be okay."

And it really felt like it would. As if now everything would be okay.

THE SHAPES IN THE CEILING had returned. Reindeer, goahtes, mountains. Ánte was lying flat on his bed, staring up. He would have stayed there for the rest of his life if he could have. What he felt inside was all he needed, nothing else.

A bright feeling. Hope.

Maybe Erik had broken up with Julia now. Maybe he had touched Ánte on purpose; maybe it had been on purpose every time.

He didn't notice Ida until she tapped his temple.

"Hellooo?" she said. "Anybody in there?"

She was crouching next to his bed, her chin propped on the mattress.

"My dad is here to help Äddnu with some fencing so I came with."

Ánte dragged himself up.

"Do they need help?"

"Nah, they'd tell us."

He nodded and leaned back against the wall. Ida sat down too and grabbed a pillow. She hugged it as if it were a stuffed animal.

"Did you end up seeing any calves?"

"Yes."

"Were they cute?"

"Super cute."

"I wish I could have been there." She smiled. "What about Erik?"

The wall was hard against his back. He squirmed, his shoulder blades catching. "What about him?"

"Was he cute?"

"I don't know what you're talking about."

"Hanna is really confused about everything you said, you know. And sad. She thinks you like somebody else." Ida let her pillow fall down in her lap. "And I think I know who."

His back hurt, his body didn't fit right against the wall. He leaned forward, then back again. One of his legs was falling asleep.

"What do you mean?"

She sighed.

"You really have no clue?"

He shook his head. His body was boiling but his skin felt cold to the touch. He was freezing. Sweating. Didn't know the difference.

"You like Erik, don't you? I just wish you could have said something before all this stuff with Hanna. It would have been a million times easier for both of you."

His body was in full rebellion now, both legs asleep. It felt as if something was moving through his upper body. A long snake. Maybe Ida would leave if he threw up on the floor.

"I can tell you feel like shit, Ánte! What's your problem? It's pretty obvious that he likes you too."

"No." Ánte got up from his bed. Tried shaking his legs back to life. His head spun from standing up. He had to close his eyes. "I'm going outside to help my dad."

"Why else do you think Julia is so wary of you? Because it's *obvious*."

He crossed his arms to stop them from shaking.

"You forget that Julia is his *girlfriend*. Girl. Chick. Woman. *That's* obvious, if anything."

He didn't tell her what Erik had told him. That he was going to break up with Julia. Or maybe he already had? Ida didn't need to know that. Not when she could use it against him.

She imitated his arm gesture.

"You seem to have forgotten that *you* had a girlfriend recently."

"Seriously, we weren't even together."

"Hanna thought so."

"Stop it."

"No, I'm not going to stop. *You* stop! Be honest for once."

Ida got off the bed and stood in front of Ánte.

"Are you in love with Erik?"

He looked down at the hooked rug beneath their feet. He could feel every single knot through his socks.

"If you don't answer, I'll leave. I don't want to be with somebody who lies and hurts my friends."

The words hit him full force. Why was it so difficult? Why couldn't he just say what he was thinking? The distance between his brain and his tongue seemed endless. It would take so much courage, he didn't know if it was even possible.

He looked up. Looked straight into her eyes.

"Yes."

"Yes?"

He could do it, would do it. All he had to do was open his mouth and say it.

"I'm in love with Erik."

He hadn't noticed the weight on his heart until it was gone. Ida pulled him close. Hugged him hard. Her embrace was soft and warm. Safe.

"I'll give you a challenge," she whispered close to his ear. "Tell somebody. It doesn't matter who. And tell Hanna you're sorry."

That was something he couldn't promise. Confessing to Ida had been hard enough. He pulled himself closer to her, gripped her shoulders hard.

"Okay?" she said. "Before the week is over. I'll text you on Sunday."

"But who do I tell? I can't just . . ."

"Just do it. You don't have your whole life."

HE WAS STANDING outside Áhkko's house. She had hung a plastic flower wreath on the front door. He counted the flowers several times while he gathered courage. Thought about what Ida had said. *Just do it.* Then he stepped up on the porch and felt the door handle.

The door was unlocked.

There was a special smell in Áhkko's house. It had always been there. A safe and warm smell—a mix of newly baked bread, tanned reindeer skins and fabric softener. And something else, hard to put your finger on. It was as if the smell eased the tension he was carrying around, the angst from Ida's challenge.

He heard Áhkko walking around upstairs. Soon her slippers shuffled toward the creaking stairs.

He glanced at the photo collage on the wall. In the lower corner was a recent picture of Ánte, a portrait. He was dressed in a gábdde. He had no idea when the picture had been taken. When he leaned closer, he noticed that Áhkko had moved the picture of the reindeer-herding dog up. She had attached it with a piece of tape and now you could see the face on the picture below. It wasn't Ánte, after all, it was that same old picture of his dad that had been partially covered by another picture. He looked like he might have been sixteen, seventeen. The lines of his face were much softer than they were now.

"Who is it?" Áhkko called from the stairs.

"Ánte," he replied.

The steps quickened.

Her arms around his upper body. She hugged him hard.

Ánte's eyes met his dad's in the photo.

"Nah," Áhkko said, letting go of him. "Le gus nälggomin?"

"Iv la," he answered. "Lev juo bårråm."

"Come and sit down anyway."

She gestured toward the kitchen, where the spring sun was shining in between beige panel curtains. Simple designs of reindeer, suns and people filled the fabric. A houseplant bloomed on the windowsill. Áhkko pulled out a green wooden chair and sat down at the table. Ánte sat next to her. The chair legs wobbled beneath him.

Should he say something now? How would he start? Áhkko interrupted his thoughts.

"Have you looked at the book again?" she asked.

"A little," he said, thinking about the torn pages.

"Well, well, I suppose it wasn't that nice for you to read that. But I would like to look at it a little more sometime."

He shrugged. Ran a finger along the edge of the table. The shapes of the pattern on the tablecloth stood up a little: you could feel it when you moved your hand over it. It calmed him.

"Men dal huomahav," Áhkko said, standing up. "Your bootlaces are done."

She disappeared from the kitchen and quickly returned with two red and blue coiled laces. Ánte took them from her. The laces were soft against the palms of his hands. He touched the tassels at the end.

"You'll look handsome at the wedding now."

"Gijtto," he said. "They turned out really nice."

"Lucky somebody is finally getting married," Áhkko said and sat down again. "So we get to see people again! It's been so long since we saw some of them. Like your ristáhttje."

Ánte nodded. He missed Lasse too.

"Do you know if he's coming to the wedding?"

Áhkko shook her head.

"I don't want to guess. But it sure would be nice if he did! He must miss you."

Ánte hoped she was right.

"Poor guy. It wasn't easy for him here."

What did she mean? Ánte remembered what Dad and his friends had said about Ruben, but he didn't remember them talking about Lasse like that. All they said was that he had met a woman from Stockholm.

Ánte didn't have a chance to ask what Áhkko meant before she continued.

"Speaking of weddings," she said. "Have you found a partner yet?"

His stomach dropped. He had almost managed to forget Ida's challenge. Was this when he was supposed to say it? Tell her. Be honest. Just do it. But he had no idea how he would make it happen. It was not as easy as Ida had made it sound.

He smiled but his voice broke.

"Not yet."

"Are there any ten-pointers in the village, or whatever you young people call it these days?"

"Only when we talk about moose."

"Aha, ah well."

"Speaking of . . . ," he began, but his voice disappeared along the way. His throat had dried up. His tongue too. He could taste the tension in his mouth.

"Well, well," Áhkko said. "You have so much to look forward to. Oh, but we had fun in Jokkmokk at the dances. But back in my day, Sámis were expected to dance only with other Sámis. Or that's what my mother thought. Now you probably run around to any of the dances."

"Uh-huh," he replied.

"Do you dance?"

"No. Never."

"That's too bad," she said. "No wonder it takes so long to find your life partner these days."

"Mm. But . . . ," he tried. Put his hands in his lap, folded them tightly. "I actually did meet someone. Kind of. I suppose. Sort of."

"What do you know! I thought so." She smiled mischievously. "And who is she?"

She. As if that were the only option. He gathered all the courage he had in his body, forced his mouth to shape the words.

"You know Erik?"

"Erik who?"

His heart thundered.

"Per-Ailo's son. He's my age."

"Yes, I know, the one who's going with Stenman's daughter."

"Right, but . . ."

Áhkko slapped her thighs. Her eyebrows shot up her forehead, creating long creases on her skin.

"You've not gone and fallen in love with a girl who's already taken?"

"What? No, but . . ."

His face burned. He would never be able to say it. Never, never, never. No matter what Ida said. She couldn't understand how this felt.

He had to work hard to pronounce every word that came out of his mouth:

"It doesn't matter. I like somebody I shouldn't like. It doesn't matter."

Áhkko looked at him for a moment.

"That's what they said about me when I got married," she said and smiled a little at something far away.

"This is different."

Silence settled over them like a blanket. Áhkko looked out the window, beyond the houses, toward the woods. The sun met her eyes. One of her hands trembled, he noticed now. She pressed her fingertips together, as if holding something tiny.

"That's how it is with love, Ánndaris. Love has always been like that."

ACCORDING TO THE CLOCK it was a few minutes after ten on Sunday morning when his phone buzzed, clattering on the porcelain counter.

Ida: *Confession check! Who did you tell??*

He sighed and put the phone back on the sink without opening the message; he'd only read the header. He spit the toothpaste foam out and rinsed his toothbrush. The taste of mint was strong in his throat.

Then he sat down on the toilet lid to think. Didn't know what to tell Ida. Several minutes passed, then several more. When the phone vibrated again, he couldn't resist opening the chat.

Ida: *I texted with Erik.*

Ánte: *What did you write? What did he say?*

She took a long time to reply, or it felt like it. The bubbles next to her profile picture never stopped bouncing.

Ida: *Eh, he might have thought I was flirting with him . . .*

She sent two emojis that were laughing so hard they were crying. It made him cry for other reasons.

Ánte: *???*

Ida: *Just asked if he was invited to the wedding. He's coming of course.*

Ánte: *Didn't he think it was weird that you asked*

Ida: *No but hellooo think about it*

Ida: *Can't wait for your wedding, how cute*

Ida: *Are you going to wear a gábdde?*

Ánte: *For real*

Ida: *Looking forward to it*

Ida: *What's your ship name? Anrik?*

Ida: *Erànte*

Ida: *No that sounds like Ferrante*

Ánte: *You have a serious problem with accents on letters*

Ida: *Erinte?*

Ida: *Ánrik is probably the best*

Ida: *Who did you tell btw?*

He swiped to get out of the conversation and put his phone in his pocket. It buzzed a few more times.

His mom stopped him outside the bathroom.

"*Whaaat?*"

"Didn't you take some pictures of Sunná and Stefan when Agnes was born? I can't find any in the computer. Thought I'd make them a gift."

He shrugged.

"If I did, they're like super old."

"That's okay, isn't it?"

Ánte sighed. Mom and technology did not mix. He didn't even want to know what she was going to do with the photos.

"They'll have really low resolution, but if you really want them . . ."

"Thank you," she said. Then she disappeared into her room.

He kept his collection of old phones in a shoe box in the closet. It was crammed in with tangled cords and headphones. He dug out a Samsung phone that he got when he was ten, had to search awhile before he found a charger.

When the phone was charged, he put his thumb on the Start button. A little melody played, then the home screen lit up. He went into the photo gallery and flipped through the pictures.

There were two pictures of Sunná and Stefan, taken on the same occasion. Sunná lying on the couch with a baby at her breast. Stefan sitting next to her, his hand on her knee. One of the photos was blurry, the other had an orange finger smudge in one corner.

The next photo was of Sunná's dad holding the newborn girl. Next to him stood his brother Lasse, who was holding a hand on his shoulder. Both men grinned into the camera.

When Ánte saw Lasse, he thought about what Áhkko had said. That it had not been easy for him here. What had she meant, exactly? Ánte didn't remember hearing anything like that before. Come to think of it, he didn't remember much about Lasse's move at all.

It occurred to him that maybe he had Lasse's number in this phone. Maybe he could contact him? They had texted now and then, hadn't they? He touched the message icon at the bottom of the screen and scrolled past conversations with Mom, Dad, Erik and other friends before he found Lasse's name.

The latest text from Lasse was from more than three years ago.

Happy birthday Ante 13 years old! Miss you Lasse

Apparently, neither Ida nor Lasse could write Ánte's name right. It made him smile, in spite of himself. He felt something warm in his stomach. But it didn't look like he had replied to the text. What an ungrateful birthday child he must have been.

Scrolling up he saw several messages with big time gaps between them.

Most often it was *Happy birthday* or *Thank you for the Christmas present. Once, Lasse had written Happy birthday from the Stockholm crew.*

The Stockholm crew? Who were they? Was it Lasse, his wife and their children that Ánte knew nothing about? They probably had a weird dialect. That strange *sje* sound they used in Stockholm. Shrill voices. They probably didn't know anything about Lasse's old life. Did they even know that they were Sámi?

Ánte shrugged off his thoughts. Where did that jealousy come from? Lasse didn't belong to him at all. They weren't even in touch anymore. But suddenly he missed him so much his chest ached.

He picked up his current phone and added Lasse's number. Would it be strange to write him now? When they had not talked for years? Lasse might not even have his number anymore. Would he need to explain who he was?

He started a new text message.

Hi, Lasse, long time no see. Just wanted to know if you're planning on coming to Sunná and Stefan's wedding? Would be fun to see you. —Ánte

He double-checked the number. Stared at the screen for a while before he hit Send.

He rarely wrote text messages anymore—everyone he talked to used Facebook Messenger. It felt strange not knowing if Lasse would even see his message.

A few hours later, he still didn't have an answer. He checked the number again. It was the right one. Maybe Lasse didn't check his phone that often. Or maybe he didn't have the same number anymore.

Ánte put his old phone back in the shoe box and shoved it in the closet. On a wooden hanger hung his gábdde. If you had a gábdde, you definitely wore it to a wedding. His chest cloth, sliehppá, lay folded in a box on the floor of the closet.

He sat down on the rug and opened the box. Moved his fingers across the colored squares, the blue cloth and the decorations in white leather. His leather boots were farther in, the old bootlaces shoved inside. He held a boot to his face, put his nose to the tanned reindeer skin. The smell made him feel safe—it reminded him of Áhkko.

The new bootlaces had not been tied to his boots yet. They were still on his desk with his schoolbooks, his papers and a bunch of junk. Clean, bright colors compared with the old ones.

He stood up and retrieved them. Swept a few candy wrappers into the trash can. He carefully untied the old laces and put them aside. Then he tied the new ones on, put his feet in the boots and started wrapping. Several times around the ankle, up a little along the leg. The laces shone bright in red and blue. He pulled tight, tied firmly, with confidence, until he was out of shoelace. He secured the tassel on the side of the boot.

Then he sat there on the floor with his leather boots on. Of all his body parts, his feet were the only ones that had found their way home.

HANNA HAD STILL not replied. But she hadn't blocked him either. He typed the text out in the phone's notes app first, edited several times. But he never did get it to sound just right. He either came off too uncertain or too confident. He changed a few words even at the very last moment.

Ánte: *I know that I'm not supposed to write to you, but Ida wants me to. She feels I have treated you badly and I agree. I'm sorry that I was so stupid and then didn't leave you alone. Still don't leave you alone. If you meant that I can't fool anybody into believing that I like girls, you may be right. At least I couldn't fool you and I also don't want to.*

Hitting Send gave him an adrenaline rush. It felt both petrifying and hopeful at the same time. It didn't really matter if she replied—even if it was a little late, he had met Ida's challenge. He had told somebody. He'd been honest.

Hanna: *That's not even what I meant. I just thought you liked somebody else and were using me to make that person jealous. I get it now.*

Ánte: *I'm sorry.*

Hanna: *Everything would have gone so much better if you'd just been honest right away. Tip: be honest next time.*

Ánte: *Yes, I know. I didn't know how to say it.*

Hanna: *There are others like you, don't you get that? It's not exactly unusual.*

Ánte: *But it feels like there aren't. At least I don't know anybody.*

Hanna: *Not exactly like you, of course. But it's not weird, it's something positive!*

Hanna: *God I get so frustrated.*

Ánte: *Sorry.*

Hanna: *You really don't get it, do you? Just be yourself. Nobody else is like you.*

He had to smile when he read her message.

Ánte: *I get that you're mad at me. But just so you know, I think you're cool and I would really like to be your friend.*

Ánte: *Or I mean nice, something like that.*

Why was it so difficult for him to express himself in writing? He rubbed his hand over his face. His cheek was hot beneath the palm of his hand.

Hanna: *I honestly don't want to see you for a while. But I doubt I'll be able to avoid it . . . but I don't have the energy to be mad at you anymore.*

Ánte: *Hope you can forgive me sometime.*

Hanna wrote for a long time. The bubbles bounced next to her picture. But when the message arrived, it was only a few words.

Hanna: *Someday, Ánte.*

SUDDENLY, THE DOOR to Ánte's room opened. Ida walked right in and started rummaging in his desk drawers.

Ánte put his phone down and dragged himself out of bed.

"What are you doing here?"

"Can I just look at the book quickly? I want to take a picture for my mom."

When she couldn't find it in his desk drawer, she started rummaging through the dresser. Before he could stop her, she'd found it.

"What did you do?" She flipped through the few pages that were still there, looked around the room for the missing ones. One page ended up outside the covers when she slammed the book down on the desk. "Hellooo?"

He shrugged.

"God, Ánte, what's wrong with you? What did you do to the pages?"

Why was everybody so irritated with him? And why did they care so much what he did? Why couldn't people just leave him alone?

He nodded toward the trash can under the desk.

Ida sighed and sat down on the desk chair. She leaned her head back and spun around a few times. Her eyes at the ceiling, she said:

"What were you expecting, really?"

"What do you mean, expecting?"

"From the book."

At first, he didn't understand what she meant. He'd not been looking for anything in particular; he'd picked up the book by mistake at the market. But the more he read, the more obvious it became that he was indeed looking for something.

"I wanted to find someone like me, I guess."

She shook her head.

"You're not going to find that in a book about racial biology. That's pretty obvious, isn't it?"

"I just got upset. About all the horrible things that happened."

"Me too! But you can't just tear everything up that upsets you and think that that will make things all right."

She picked up the book again, flipped through a few pages. Rolled the chair over to Ánte and put the book in his lap.

"Here is somebody like you. And me."

In front of him was the picture of Ánnda from the side. Ida had thought the same thing Ánte thought when Áhkko told him about the family connection. But could that really be enough? Ánte was really different. He traced his finger along the hair, forehead, nose, chin.

"You even look alike," Ida said.

"You think?"

"Umm, yes!"

He studied the picture more closely. He felt like he was missing somebody he had never met.

"But you don't know what he was like," he said. "We didn't know him."

"No, but you won't find anybody more like you in this book."

He looked at the photo for a long time. She was right, of course, but it still made him feel sad.

"It just feels like they might not have liked me. If they knew."

Ida blew air out of her nose, made a sad face.

"Ánte," she said, drawing his name out. "Imagine that you had a great-grandchild. You would care about that child. And love it, even if you'd never met."

"I can't know that."

"Yes, you can," she said. "Because that child would be your family."

"I suppose."

"Ánnda and Siggá *are* your family. As are your parents. And Áhkko. And me. It never ends." She wheeled closer, until the chair hit the edge of the bed. "Get it? Nobody can take us from you. Ever."

"Sure?"

"Sure."

She put her feet in Ánte's lap. He picked at the sole of her foot through her sock until she started giggling. Her laughter made him smile. The pressure started easing.

"Do you know what I did today?" he asked.

She shook her head.

"I confessed to somebody."

"Who?"

"Hanna."

Ida smiled but for once she didn't say anything. Instead, she lifted her feet from Ánte's lap, put them against the edge of the bed and pushed, making the chair roll to the desk. She bent over and picked up the trash can.

"Do you have tape?"

"In the top drawer."

Roll of tape in one hand, she turned the trash can upside down. Then she sat down on the floor with the book in front of her, flattened the wrinkled pages as best she could. Page by page she taped them together again.

HE HANDED ÁHKKO the shredded book. She took it, shook her head a little.

"It broke?"

"Yes."

She touched the pieced-together pages in the middle of the book. A page nearby fell out and sailed to the floor.

"It was just a few pages," Ánte said. "That fell out."

"What do you mean 'fell out'?"

He shook his head. Picked up the page and gave it to Áhkko. Ignored the faces that stared up at him.

"We tried to fix it. I thought maybe you'd want it."

She gave him a dubious look. Then she shook her head too.

"Let's look together."

They sat down close together on the couch, the book in Áhkko's lap.

"What kind of a man was Harald?" Ánte asked.

"A racial biologist. A doctor, I suppose, to begin with. In the beginning, in the early twentieth century, racial biology was big in Sweden."

"What was even the point of it?"

"Well, that . . ." Áhkko said. "For some reason, they wanted to prove that Swedes were a superior race to Sámis, Finns and other people. Not that I think they ever came to any intelligent conclusions."

"It sounds like Nazi Germany."

"That's right, the Nazis in Germany were inspired by Swedish racial biologists."

"For real?"

"For real."

Áhkko opened the book and picked up her own photos. They compared them with Harald Lundgren's pictures. A totally different perspective. The very same people.

"You see," she said, pointing. "He clearly chose which pictures to include. In his book he used only the photos that supported his theory of how Sámis looked."

Many of the Sámis that Lundgren had photographed looked weary. They all had a distinctive look that Ánte could not see in himself. Ida had been right. How could he possibly find himself in a bunch of pictures selected by a racial biologist? A collection where the most important thing was appearance.

"Not all Sámis look the same," Áhkko said. "Or any other people. God, no. It's nonsense, measuring people like this."

Ánte looked at her.

"Were you racially examined?"

She shook her head.

"How about your parents?"

"I don't know. We never talked about things like that. It's news to me that my father's parents were photographed, but it doesn't surprise me."

She pulled out the photo of Ánnda and Siggá that Ánte had left in the book. Apparently, Ida hadn't taped that picture back in. Áhkko gave him a quizzical look.

He scratched the area by his thumbnail. Sighed.

"I tore out the pages. I just got so angry."

"At whom?"

"At everything."

Áhkko stroked the back of his hand. Separated his fingers so he couldn't scratch.

"I don't think it helps to tear things up," she said. "Or throw things out. No matter how much it hurts, we must remember." Áhkko sounded just like Ida.

"But why?"

"It's a part of our history. It's already been forgotten by so many people."

Ánte leaned his head against the back of the couch. He didn't know, suddenly, if he should breathe through his nose or his mouth. As if he'd ever thought about it before.

"What are you thinking about?" Áhkko asked.

"May I have that picture? The one with Ánnda and Siggá?"

"Of course you may," Áhkko said. "It's your book."

He picked up the cut-out picture. It was soft in his hand.

"I, um, I wondered . . ." He hesitated. "Is it still painful for you?"

She shook her head.

"Not usually. But I think about my parents a lot. But I would have missed them now regardless of how things had turned out." She looked at him closely. "Is it still painful for you?"

He didn't know how to explain it. He was afraid Áhkko wouldn't understand. Because he had already tried telling her about Erik once before.

Instead he just nodded. Áhkko let out a deep sigh.

"You're just a child," she said. "You should not have to feel pain."

"I just don't know how to *be*," he said. "No matter what I do, there is always somebody who thinks it's wrong."

Áhkko shook her head.

"There is no right or wrong," she said. "You choose that for yourself. When I met your áddjá, I chose to disregard what people said."

"What do you mean? What did people say?"

"My mother wanted me to marry a Sámi man instead. A reindeer herder, preferably. But if I had not followed my heart, you would not have been here today. And we would not have had our amazing family. Do you know what I mean?"

Ánte knew that Áddjá had not been Sámi, but he had never understood that it meant that there had been a conflict.

"I think so. I'm just afraid that I will lose something. That I will have to choose."

Áhkko squeezed his hand. Maybe she understood more than he thought.

"That's exactly what my parents believed. They thought I would give up the reindeer and turn Swedish just because I married Åke, but that didn't happen. Nobody can take our culture away from us. And they really tried!"

Ánte had never heard Áhkko talk about this before. He realized how little he actually knew about her life.

She squeezed his hand again.

"Is this about the love you mentioned when we were together last time?"

He could only nod.

Áhkko put her arms around him. She was warm, smelled safe. A big feeling swelled behind his ribs. He had not cried in front of Áhkko since he was little. But he couldn't stop it now.

Or hide it.

"Sweetheart." She wiped her rough finger under his eye. "I have learned at least two things from my time on this earth. The first is that no matter what happens, most things usually turn out all right in the end."

He put his head on her shoulder.

"What is the other thing?"

She brushed his bangs from his forehead, looked him in the eye, held her hand to his cheek.

"That nothing is greater than love. Neither fear, nor hate."

THE NEW CHURCH in Jokkmokk towered in front of them. The creamy-white walls shone softly in the sun, the steeple pointed straight up in the sky. Just then the church bells began to ring.

Ánte's mom opened the gate and let Ánte and his dad walk in ahead of her. More people were following behind them; some were ahead, already on their way into the church. His mom stopped to hug people she knew. Ánte just said hello, then looked away so he wouldn't have to talk. He looked for Erik but didn't see him. Almost everybody was dressed in gábde—mostly blue or black with bright details in red, yellow and green. Some wore other colors, contemporary colors, colors that would make Áhkko raise her eyebrows. Purple, turquoise, even floral patterns.

A couple of little girls ran past Ánte toward the church. Their gábde were pink and glittery, like princess dresses. Ánte's mom wrinkled her nose when she saw them.

"I think it's okay to experiment," she whispered in Ánte's ear, "but there's a limit, no?"

"I saw a man with a floral gábdde once," he said. He didn't know why he told her this. Just wanted a reaction. "A student at Sámi school made it."

His mother's eyes narrowed.

"Soon we'll have no traditions left."

As soon as they stepped inside the church doors, they were greeted by people they knew. Most of their relatives were there. They hugged, shook hands, said buoris and somebody asked how school was. *Fine, thank you.* Áhkko was talking to her siblings. She smiled at Ánte and gently touched his shoulder.

Ida nudged him from behind. She nodded toward the church benches.

"I saw a good-looking guy over there," she said. "Like *crazy* good-looking."

He was about to turn and look in the benches behind Ida but managed to refrain.

"Maybe you should go sit there then?"

She rolled her eyes. Typical Ida to roll her eyes like that.

"Or you just go back there and try to pick him up," she said.

Ánte looked around but nobody seemed to have reacted to what she said.

They walked farther into the church. Ánte and his parents sat down on the right side, squeezed into a row. He ended up on the aisle.

The hall filled up with people. A low murmuring and the sound of Sámi boots on the floor. He kept a lookout for people he knew, or at least recognized. Or just Erik.

Then he saw him on the other side of the aisle. Ánte turned to talk to the relatives sitting behind him but he kept glancing over toward the other side. Erik was flipping through the Lule Sámi book of psalms. A strand of hair had fallen down his forehead. The light from the church window made his hair glow white at the edges.

And then he looked up. His gaze burned right through Ánte, as if he had already known exactly where he sat.

The doors in the back of the church opened. All the guests turned around, a long inhalation spread through the room. Then: silence.

Sunná and Stefan lit up the church when they stepped inside. She was wearing a long burgundy gábdde. On her chest: a large, round silver pin. It shone in the soft light, made a tinkling sound when she walked. In her hair she wore a bridal crown and a thin, white bridal veil. She looked like a queen.

Stefan was also wearing a gábdde, a Jokkmokk gábdde, like Ánte's. It was shorter than Sunná's. Under it, he wore brown suede pants. Around his neck and over his chest, he wore a blue chest cloth.

Stefan was holding Sunná's hand tightly, as if afraid that she might vanish.

They walked up to the altar, both of them with big smiles on their faces. It felt like no two faces could possibly express more joy. Stefan wiped the corner of his eye. Sunná laughed softly.

A jolt went through Ánte's body. A warm feeling filled his chest, something wet rolled down his chin. He didn't recognize this feeling, wasn't prepared. It overwhelmed him. He quickly wiped his tears; the blue fabric of his sleeve was rough against his cheek.

Would he ever have what Sunná and Stefan had? A love so natural to celebrate. A love that everybody found beautiful.

When he turned around, the first thing he saw was Erik's gaze.

A woman yoiked when the newly married couple walked out of the church. The notes reverberated through the hall, thundered through his entire body. A sense of wonder filled the air. Ánte wanted to lie down in it. Feel it in his hair, wrapped around his fingers.

A murmur spread when the guests stood up. Shoes clip-clopped on the floor, children ran between the legs of adults. Ánte's legs were not adult, just very weak when he stood up. He looked for Erik in the crowd but could no longer see him. His mom put her hand on his back and steered him along. His dad was walking a few steps ahead.

His mom draped a red plaid shawl around her shoulders as they walked out of the church.

"They're serving food in the community center now."

"Let's drive," his dad said.

"For real?" Ánte stared at him. "It's like three meters away."

His dad sighed.

"You need to learn to count before you get to have an opinion."

Ánte scoffed.

"I was kidding."

"Me too. Come on."

Ánte walked slowly. He ended up several meters behind his mom and dad. Crazy that they couldn't even walk for a few minutes. And it's not like they didn't have to walk to the car anyway.

"You're walking in the wrong direction."

He turned around. Couldn't keep from smiling. His grin spread across his entire face.

"Right. I told my mom and dad, but they wanted to take *the car*."

Erik laughed. He was bursting with color even though the rest of the world was gray.

"Walk with me, then."

Ánte called in the direction of his parents:

"Go on without me, I'm walking with Erik."

They both turned around and looked at him. He couldn't hear what they said. They just kept walking. His mom's shawl fluttered on her back. He shrugged.

“They don’t actually seem to care.”

“Let’s go, then,” Erik said and turned around.

“Do your parents know that you left?”

“They manage without me. And they have a car.”

Ánte laughed. There was a brightness inside his body. When he looked at Erik he glimpsed a light in his eyes too.

THE COMMUNITY CENTER was packed with people. Ánte could hardly breathe. The room was stuffy and warm. His chest felt squeezed. There was a board with table-seating charts, the name of a guest by each chair. He looked for his name, found it on one of the tables far away. Erik's name was nowhere close.

He inhaled through his nostrils, looked out over the nicely set tables. Made eye contact with Erik, who pointed to his own spot. Ánte nodded and pointed to his. Erik raised his hand as if waving goodbye. As if they wouldn't see each other again, even though they were in the same room.

Ánte made his way past all the people, ended up on the wrong side of the table from where he was supposed to sit. Saw his name on the other side and walked around. The bottom of his feet were beginning to hurt. The Sámi boots were hard on the soles of his feet.

"Well, well, if it isn't Ánndaris."

There stood a man dressed in a gábdde that looked like his own. It took a second for Ánte to recognize him. He looked much older than when he had last seen him.

"Lasse!"

They hugged. Ánte closed his eyes for a moment. Lasse patted his back.

"Oh my," he said. "I haven't seen you since you were this tall."

He lowered one hand, held it at knee height. Ánte laughed and shook his head. This time his smile came naturally.

"You used to buy me that special kind of juice," he said. "I remember. The green kind, in a bottle. Cactus flavor, I think."

"That's right!" Lasse raised a finger, knocked on his forehead. "What a memory you have, lad."

"Of course, I remember."

Should he mention that he had tried to reach Lasse? It felt a little embarrassing now for some reason.

Maybe it was better to pretend like he hadn't.

When Lasse smiled, his whole face scrunched up. His eyebrows were thick and dark; they hung down over his eyelids. His eyes turned into thin folds, barely visible among the wrinkles when he laughed.

"You were a special child," he said. "You probably still are."

"Hm."

Ánte looked at his boots. Didn't quite understand what Lasse meant.

"I've thought about you a lot," Lasse said.

Ánte looked up. Lasse's smile was still wide, but maybe not quite as cheerful. His eyes had gotten bigger, his smile had lost its grip around the edges.

"After you moved?"

Lasse pulled out a chair and sat down. He picked at the thick napkin folded next to his plate. Ánte looked for the seating placement card to make sure he sat down in the right spot. That was when he realized that they had the seats next to each other. He was sitting so close that he could hear Lasse breathing. His breath was hoarse, scratchy.

"Some southerner moved into your house after you left," Ánte continued. "Somebody who thought Sámis were cool as hell, and snow, and northern lights, all that. It wasn't great living across from him."

He didn't know where his words came from. Something about Lasse's silence forced them out. He reached for the pitcher and poured some water in his glass. Leaned back, took a mouthful.

"One day in the fall, we found him behind the shed, taking a picture of the hide we'd nailed up after slaughter. No idea what he was after. But the house is empty now."

Lasse was still quiet, not looking at Ánte.

"Do you still live in Stockholm?"

"Yes."

"Dad was right, then."

Lasse nodded, looked up at him, then down again. Something had changed. There was an entirely new feeling in the air. As if things were happening far, far away.

Or maybe inside.

"What else did he say?" Lasse asked.

"What?"

"About me."

Ánte stopped in the middle of a breath.

"Nothing, I think."

Should he tell the truth? What his dad and his dad's friends had said about Lasse's woman in Stockholm—the woman he had presumably gotten pregnant? It was probably better to ask.

"Why did you move?"

Maybe he would finally find out who *the Stockholm crew* was. If the rumors were true.

Lasse looked up. He smiled a little, but only with the corner of his mouth.

"For Ruben."

A sudden jolt of jealousy shot through him.

"Is Ruben your son?"

Lasse shook his head.

"Ruben is my husband. We've been married for ten years now."

The entire room turned quiet. Glasses stopped clinking, people stopped talking, the heart inside his chest stopped beating.

But only for a second. Then the world started up again. Ánte drank from his glass. Wiped some sweat from his forehead.

"You mean Ruben from town?"

"Yes," Lasse said. "He couldn't join me this time."

"Ah."

Ánte picked at the skin flap next to his thumbnail. It stung; the skin was red after all the picking.

"Why did you have to move?"

His words came out more quietly than he had intended. Lasse frowned. Ánte had to ask again. His voice sounded strange, uneven. His throat hurt.

Lasse looked like he was laughing but no sound came out.

"You know . . . ," he said. "In my generation it was not super acceptable for men to be with other men. At least not in the villages. It was easier down south."

More and more pressure built in his chest.

"But you had reindeer," Ánte said. He took too much water in his mouth, coughed it up. "You were a part of the Sámi village. What happened to your reindeer?"

Lasse balled his hands into fists. They were gnarly, his skin spotted. He shook his head.

"Ruben, he . . . he had a very hard time."

"Was it easier to just leave everything and move?"

Ánte poured more water in his glass. The pitcher was almost empty.

People had started finding their way to the table. A few were sitting at the other end, laughed out loud at something he couldn't hear.

"Love, you know." Lasse smiled, but only with his mouth. "Love is like a drug. There's nothing you won't do. You'll experience it when you get older."

Ánte looked down at the table, shook his head.

"I could never leave all this."

Lasse's mouth was open, but it took a while before he spoke.

"You don't have to, do you?"

The sliehppá was choking him. It felt too tight suddenly. Ánte pulled at it. The collar sat like iron around his neck.

"You're Anders's only boy. Of course you'll take over after him."

The belt was too tight too, dug into his stomach.

"I will," he said.

"There is nothing that says you have to move just to move," Lasse said. "It was different back then. Who says you can't find love nearby?"

"But why didn't you tell people? Everybody thinks you met a girl down there."

"I know," Lasse said. "I let them believe that."

"Does Áhkko know this?"

"Your áhkko?" He looked confused. "No, I haven't told anybody."

"She said something about how it had not been easy for you here."

Lasse nodded, "It might have been obvious."

Ánte moved his hand over his face, then through his hair. Swallowed, swallowed.

"You could have told me. Did you really have to move?"

"It was very bad there for a while. I was afraid I'd lose Ruben if we stayed."

Lasse looked small and fragile there in his chair, not his usual self. He looked like he might break if you just touched his ear or his collarbone.

"Lose him?"

"He wasn't well. It wasn't any easier with people talking. I don't know why they couldn't just leave him alone."

"You could have told me. Only me."

"Ánndaris, you were a child."

Ánte's face was burning hot. He couldn't stay here; he was losing control of his feelings. He shoved his chair out behind him and stood up. The waitresses had started bringing the appetizers. Lasse looked at him. His face was broken, the creases going every which way, like cracks.

"Are you okay?" Lasse asked.

Ánte accidentally bumped one of the waitresses as he left. A dab of a light cream sauce ended up on her black sleeve. She said something but he couldn't hear it. He was already close to the exit.

THE COOL AIR was a relief. Ánte took a deep breath and undid his belt. He threw it across his shoulder and moved the dark fabric up and down, tried to get some cool air in under it. A breeze swept across his stomach. There was still pressure on his throat.

He moved his hands behind his neck, undid the two small buttons of the sliehppá. It was looser now.

"Are you standing here getting undressed?"

The voice made every hair on his body stand up. Ánte turned around, and there he was. Erik.

"This gábdde feels like fucking armor."

Erik nodded. He looked at the belt hanging over Ánte's shoulder.

"I know. It's always nice to get it off when you get home. But I see that you couldn't wait."

The heaviness in Ánte's body began to seep out. Erik smiled at the ground, his eyes on Ánte's leather boots, "Are you going to undo your bootlaces too?"

Ánte raised his eyebrows.

"Want me to?"

"That would be something."

"It feels like I have tape wound tightly around my ankles."

"Right. Might as well take the whole boot off." Erik bent down and started unwinding his own shoelaces. One loop after the other. Ánte stared.

"Do you really have it in you to rewind those?"

Erik stopped, looked at him.

"I'm not going to."

There seemed to be something else in Erik's voice, something other than the words he was saying. Something burning. What were they doing?

"Okay?"

Ánte moved his hand across his forehead, through his hair.

"You have something in your hair?"

"What?"

"You do that a lot."

He dropped his arm.

Erik kicked his first boot off. His bootlace slithered across the ground like a long snake. The pattern changed colors, lit up on the asphalt.

"Finally," he said, grabbing his ankle. He was only wearing a sock on that foot now. It was red with white hearts. Through the hearts went black arrows.

"Nice." Ánte nodded at Erik's foot.

Erik tilted his head and smiled.

"I know."

The other boot came off, landed on the ground.

"Your turn," Erik said, nodding at Ánte's body.

It caught fire as if on command. Was Erik flirting?

"You know we're right outside the front door?"

"You're not going to strip naked, are you?"

Ánte opened his mouth, then closed it. All his words were stuck in his throat. Where were they going with all this?

"Nobody ever died from seeing a guy without shoes," Erik said.

"This might be the first time. Just wait until my mom sees us."

"Let's leave, then."

"You're not wearing shoes."

"I've gone without shoes since I was like three years old."

Ánte looked up at the sky. It felt dizzyingly vast, and he felt so little. His feet almost lifted off the ground.

"You already took your belt off," Erik said. "And me my shoes. We might as well take off."

"But where to?"

"There must be a place for people like us too."

Ánte's body tensed. He focused on the ground under the soles of his feet.

"People like us?"

"Sámi guys tired of wearing gábde, I guess."

Ánte shook his head. He felt heat under his eyelids. He swallowed. Something was happening inside him. He swallowed again, forced it down.

"Let's go to the lake," Erik said.

He nodded toward the road. Ánte rolled up his belt. The wind swept through his gábdde, cooled his skin. Erik carried his shoes in his hand.

"It feels a little strange to celebrate love in a church that took everything we believe away from us," Erik said when they had started walking.

Ánte looked at him.

"What do you mean?"

"I can't stop thinking about the fact that we don't belong there. Why am I the only one thinking about this? I'll never get married in the Swedish church."

There was gravel under his shoes, on the asphalt. It looked like Erik was flexing his feet so they wouldn't hurt.

"But that was so long ago," Ánte said. "A lot of people are Christian today."

"That's exactly what I mean. It's horrible that so many people are Christians when it wasn't their choice; they were forced into it."

"But not the people who are alive now."

Ánte hardly knew why he was arguing like this. He knew what Erik meant—he just didn't like that he said it.

"Indirectly. Their forefathers, your and my forefathers, were made to believe that way. With force." Something shifted in Erik's face. He closed his eyes, a wrinkle appeared on his forehead. "I just think it's sick that nobody cares about that anymore. That we read psalms translated into Sámi as if it's a good thing. It makes me sick to think about it."

Now they could see Dálvvadisjávrásj in front of them. There were almost no people on the beach. A woman walking by with a black dog looked at Erik's red feet. Houses stood in rows along the beach with windows facing the lake. Ánte didn't want to stop there. He kept walking. Erik followed behind him.

The snow had melted and the ice had started breaking up, leaving the surface of the water open. The lake glittered from the wind in the waves.

They followed a walking path and entered the woods on the other side of the lake. There was no beach here, not really, the trees came down almost to the water. Erik dropped his shoes on the ground. Ánte squirmed, tugged at the fabric of his gábdde.

"Where does it hurt the most?" Erik asked.

In his heart, chest, stomach. In his whole entire body.

"My neck," Ánte said, moving his hand to the sliehppá. "But I already unbuttoned it."

"Did it help at all?"

Ánte shrugged and tried to reach the chest cloth inside the gábdde. His arms were not long enough, the cloth strained at the elbows.

"Come here," Erik said. "I'll help you."

Ánte took a few steps closer to Erik. Felt his breath on his cheek. A soft, thin touch. Erik's fingers moved inside the thick material. His fingertips were warm on Ánte's back, made his skin shiver.

"Are you cold?" Erik asked. Quietly, close to Ánte's ear.

Another shiver through his body.

"No. Or, maybe a little."

Erik backed up a few steps.

"I can't reach, either. You have to turn around."

Ánte turned his back to Erik and looked through the trees and out over the lake. Erik's hands wandered in under the cloth, up over his back. The sliehppá strings were loosened, the pressure lessened.

Ánte moved his hand into the V-shaped chest opening of the gábdde and tugged at the cloth. The lace came off. His naked skin turned cold. He held the sliehppá in front of him.

"Where do I put this?"

Erik was looking at Ánte's chest when he answered.

"Put it on top of my shoes so it won't get dirty."

Ánte nodded at Erik's feet.

"I didn't know you cared about dirt."

"This is a sock." Erik lifted his foot. "The sliehppá is a work of art."

He bent down and moved his boots apart, positioning them as if they were a rack. Ánte put his sliehppá on top of them. It lay a little lopsided, one edge hanging down in the brush.

"Nice, isn't it?" Erik said behind him.

"Uh-huh."

Ánte's sore neck had been liberated, but the pressure on his chest was still there. It didn't feel like he expected. A sense of loss burned in his stomach. A part of him lay there in the blueberry brush. Who was he now?

Just a boy in blue clothing.

"Sometimes I wish," Erik said, "that I wasn't so tied up in all this."

Ánte's eyebrows felt heavy . . . as did his lower lip. How could he say that? Nothing was more important than this.

"What?"

"Some people leave all this because they can't handle it anymore."

The surface of the water moved restlessly. Something was happening down below.

"You can't just decide to be somebody else," Ánte said. He tried to ignore the war inside.

Erik's voice was sharper now.

"You are whoever you want to be, Ánte."

Something stung in the corner of his eye. He tried to stiffen his lips, stop them from trembling. It felt like Erik was trying to take something away from him.

"Does that mean that you are who you want to be?" Ánte asked.

Erik's eyes were as hard as rocks. Ánte wished he would stop looking at him. Didn't want Erik's eyes to touch his skin with that look. Suddenly so cold on his body.

"I don't know. How would I know when I don't even have a chance to try?"

"Well, try then. Try whatever you want."

Erik stood there in silence. The entire forest was silent. Only the lake and the wind cried softly behind their backs. Maybe Erik could feel it because he turned away. Ánte looked at his red socks in the blueberry brush. White hearts, black arrows.

One of the hearts was Ánte's, and it was pierced by an arrow.

He bent over and picked up his sliehppá, brushed it off and held it tightly to his chest. He buttoned it around his neck, shoved the fabric down inside the gábdde. He couldn't tie it himself, the fabric bunched, hung off-center. He put his belt around his waist and tightened it. Everything was uncomfortable, nothing was right.

"I would never have wanted to leave," he said. "Why does everybody talk about leaving?"

"What do you mean, everybody?"

"I met Lasse at the wedding. Our old neighbor. He moved to Stockholm when I was little. Sold the reindeer and took off."

"It doesn't have anything to do with you."

"But why can't people stay? Why can't anybody just stay?"

Erik's face was darker than before.

"I don't know what your problem is, Ánte."

The arrow shot through his body, came out through his back.

"I don't know what your problem is either."

Erik's mouth was a hard line. Ánte wished he could be just as hard, but he was coming apart, his mouth falling open, everything trembling, everything shaking.

He didn't want Erik to see him like this, but he couldn't get away.

"Hey," Erik said. "We can talk if you want to."

"About *what*?" Ánte snapped. Wiped the corner of his mouth.

"Whatever you want."

"I have nothing to say."

"I think you do."

Erik took a few steps toward him. Ánte's eyes went to his feet, the socks, the hearts. It was too much. The sight hit him full force in the stomach.

"Ánte."

Erik pronounced his name as if it was fragile, as if it might break if you just raised your voice. It was true. Ánte felt like he might break if somebody just touched him.

Then again, he was probably already broken.

The world was blurry, his eyelids felt huge, heavy to lift. He didn't see Erik coming up to him. But he felt it, everywhere. In his heart, in his stomach, in his knees, buckling. Across his back, because that's where Erik's hands were. Again.

Ánte let him. He didn't have the energy to think anymore, didn't have the power to resist. Erik hugged him gently. His shoulder got wet under Ánte's nose.

"I don't want to leave," Ánte said. His voice was thick from crying. "I don't want to, I don't want to, I don't want to."

Erik hushed him.

"I know, Ánte."

He held him tighter. Ánte forced his body to relax, Erik carried him. He wouldn't drown, couldn't drown. Erik carried him now. Nothing else mattered.

A loud bark. An agitated woman's voice.

"What's going on?"

Erik removed his arms. Ánte blinked with his heavy eyelids, thick and swollen.

"It's okay," Erik told the woman.

She was standing in the middle of the trail, clutching the leash of her black dog. The dog threw itself at Ánte and Erik but couldn't quite reach.

The woman threw a skeptical glance at Erik's shoes in the brush, at his socks, at Ánte, who was turning away from her, looking down at the ground.

The dog tried to throw itself at Erik again. It barked hysterically.

"Get out of here!"

The woman pulled her dog behind her and kept moving along the trail. When she was out of sight, Erik let the air out of his lungs.

"Do we look like drug addicts, or something?"

Ánte laughed quietly. The corners of his mouth felt tight. His face had dried up from the tears.

"Hard to know," Ánte said. "But I'd say you've been acting like you're a little high all day."

And just like that, Erik was back with Ánte, his hands grabbing Ánte's shoulders. Ánte's body collapsed—but somehow, he was still standing. Erik's lips were right next to his, his pupils so large that the color around them had almost disappeared. A thin, brown edge. He leaned forward a little more, until their noses touched. Breathing was impossible.

Ánte's body shut down, quit—everything froze but his heart, a heart that was almost beating a hole through his ribs.

"Let's go back," Erik said.

ÁNTE'S MOM AND HELENE were standing in front of the entry to the community center. Ánte's mom was facing away from them, her phone to her ear.

Helene saw them immediately. "Where have you been so long?"

"We needed fresh air," Erik said. "It got too hot and crowded in there."

"You could have said something. It's not that hard."

Erik looked at her.

"Mom, I didn't even sit at your table. You were probably talking to Anna-Karin or somebody."

Her voice hardened.

"Don't be so high and mighty, young man. Where are your shoes?"

The door opened behind them and a man came out. He looked up and met Ánte's eyes.

Lasse.

Lasse's eyes swept over Erik and Erik's red socks, before returning to Ánte. Lasse looked like he was smiling a little, but before Ánte could tell for sure, he turned away. Ánte brushed his hand over his gábdde, straightened the fabric. Maybe Lasse understood.

Ánte's mom waved at Lasse. She ended her phone conversation and slipped the phone in her purse.

"Well, hello," she said. "It's been a long time!"

They hugged awkwardly and exchanged a few words before she asked Lasse to stop by the house for coffee. He said thank you, that he might look in on them later, and gave Ánte one last look before he disappeared toward his car.

Ánte's mom grabbed his arm. He looked down, away, anywhere but at her.

"Let's go."

"See you," Erik said.

Ánte couldn't even answer before his mom dragged him away.

"What have you *done*? It looks like you've been crying your eyes out."

She put her hand on his chest, by the gap in the material, straightened the sliehppá that had bunched up. Fixed the collar. He made a face.

"I haven't done anything."

She tried to make eye contact.

"Did something happen? Was somebody mean to you?"

"*Mean*?"

"I don't understand what's going on."

"Whatever," he said, but she didn't seem to be listening.

"Was it something that Erik did?"

"Erik didn't do anything."

"I am starting to wonder if Erik might be a bad influence on you."

"For real, Mom . . ."

His dad was waiting in the car. Ánte climbed in behind the passenger seat.

"Where were they?" his dad asked when his mom sat down next to him.

"I don't know. He doesn't want to tell me."

The way they talked made him feel like a child. As if they didn't think he could understand what they were saying. He sat quietly, but he wanted them to know that he could hear them. He ached with irritation.

Jokkmokk disappeared outside the window, tree by tree lined up along the country road.

"Ánte," his mom said. "I wish you would take a break from Erik for a while."

He could not stay quiet any longer.

"What the hell are you talking about?"

His mom turned around, her hair flowing down the back of the seat.

"Since you and Erik started spending so much time together, you've not really been yourself."

"What? We've been friends since we were kids."

She turned to face forward again.

"What's he even done? What have *I* done? I don't understand what your problem is."

"Not that tone," she said. "You would never have talked to me like this before. You've really changed."

He balled his hands and pushed them down in the seat. Looked at his dad, the cramped grip on the steering wheel. His face looked like it was chiseled out of rock.

"Maybe it's not good," his dad said, "if people get the wrong impression about you."

Ánte pushed his hands even harder into the seat. A red pattern appeared on his skin.

"The wrong impression?"

His dad glanced at his mom. She hesitated before she opened her mouth.

"When you spend as much time with another boy as you do, rumors begin to spread."

He put his hand on the back of his dad's seat.

"Dad hangs out with his old-man friends all the time. I don't get the difference."

"You don't spend as much time with Máhttu and Juhán as you used to. And what happened to Hanna? It's only Erik now."

He sank back in his seat. Tried to control his breathing.

"It's not true," he said.

"We don't believe that you . . . ," his mother began. She cleared her throat. "But other people are starting to imagine things. What are we going to tell them when they ask? Huh?"

His eyes were still big and warm. Sand had started collecting in the corners of his eyes. He wiped it away.

"It's just for your own sake," she continued. "And the family."

"Then it's not *just*."

"Excuse me?"

"You said it was just for my own sake. But apparently, it's also for the sake of the family."

"Ánte." She sighed. "I can't do this anymore."

His dad moved his hand from the steering wheel and rested it on his mom's seat. She put her hand in his. His mother looked tired, her face older than usual.

"Your mom is right," his dad said. "Don't be so hard on her."

His body was not big enough to hold all this anger. It pounded and hammered. Ánte wanted to kick the seat in front of him, kick until his mom felt the pounding in her back and got upset. Like you did when you were a kid. When you didn't know better.

For the rest of the ride, they were all quiet. The silence hurt his ears; he wanted to scream to break it. When they parked outside the house, his phone dinged.

Ida: *Ánterik, I didn't even think about that. That way there's room for both your names.*

IT HAPPENED A HUNDRED years ago. But it was still there inside of him. In his clothes, his gábdde. In his skeleton, his skin, his blood. Somebody else's pain had become his. It happened a hundred years ago, but it wasn't over. The abuse. The ideas of how a Sámi *should* look, how a Sámi *should* be. He had been cheated. They had all been cheated. But it wasn't their fault, he knew now.

He sat on his bed and looked at the gábdde, which he had flung down on the rug. He had only just taken it off, but now he longed to put it back on. His body was missing something. He picked up the gábdde again, held the rough fabric in his hand. Thick, dark, blue. It billowed in his arms. He traced the opening of the chest cloth with his finger, up toward the collar. Looked at the stitches keeping it together. Áhkko had sewn his gábdde. She was always meticulous; without your gábdde, Áhkko said, you were not the same.

He had never understood it, not until now.

He hugged the gábdde, lowered his chin and smelled it. The smell was familiar but also new, a combination of home and forest, wind, lake, moss. Early summer smells. And, if he wasn't imagining it: the smell of Erik.

His head disappeared under the fabric, found its way through the opening. His hair caught static. He reached up and swept his hand over his forehead, wrestled his arm into the right sleeve. The material fell into place. He pulled it down over his chest and stomach. Instead of his sliehppá, his white T-shirt peeked out from under it.

His upper body was warm now. It felt safe. Nothing was uncomfortable. He lay down on his side and pulled his knees to his stomach. The gábdde was like a blanket around him; he didn't need anything else, felt bad because he had longed to be out of it earlier.

One arm rested on the mattress. He looked at the three lines along the bottom of the sleeve. Three colors—red, yellow and blue. Like a rainbow. Only a few colors missing.

He thought about how hard it had been when Lasse told him why he moved. But it wasn't Lasse's fault, not really. He just wished that there would have been somebody who stayed.

A feeling had rooted itself inside. This was his home, his culture. Why should he have to adapt? He knew that what Erik had said in the woods was partially true. But maybe it didn't have to be? Maybe you didn't have to be so confined.

His dad had said that people might get the wrong impression about Ánte. It probably wasn't even wrong. Maybe they were just starting to understand who he really was. He didn't have it in him to worry about it anymore.

His eyelashes were wet, sticking together when he closed his eyes. He didn't care. Didn't even have the energy to lift his hand, didn't need consolation. His bones felt heavy on the mattress.

He wanted to lie exactly like this, in a warm caress. The feeling held him, rocked him, calmed his muscles. His breathing slowed; his thoughts turned confident, clear. This was where he belonged.

Ánnda and Siggá were his ancestors. His blood. He had the right to this life, this culture. The roots went deep into the soil and he didn't want to cut them. No matter what others thought, he would always belong here.

Nobody else got to decide who he should be. Only him.

THEY WERE STANDING in front of the birch forest, Ánte and Ida. He held the photo in his hand. The lake had woken up next to them, the trees were stretching in the sun. This time the place looked much more like the picture they had brought. Neither of them said anything, but Ánte could tell Ida saw it too.

Now he could sense them, the people. The ones who had stood here before him. It was just a muted feeling, but it was there. A link between now and then. Could they somehow feel him and Ida too? he wondered.

He crouched next to the tree trunks. Took a key chain from his coat pocket and began to scrape in the dirt next to the roots. The soil opened for him.

In the hole, he put the picture of Ánnda and Siggá, taped together next to each other. He carefully covered them with soil. His fingers turned black from the dirt.

Now the ground would never forget. They had left something behind.

THE PHONE VIBRATED on the kitchen table. Ánte put the sandwich on his plate, licked a few crumbs from his fingertips. The phone was warm in his hand, the words so soft.

Erik: *How are you?*

Next to the message, Erik's profile picture in a little bubble. Ánte looked at it for a long time. Spelled each individual letter out.

Ánte: *Good, I think.*

Three dots next to Erik's picture.

Erik: *Where does it hurt the most?*

Ánte noticed that he was smiling. He touched the corner of his mouth, paused before he wrote.

His mother was moving around by the sink. The plates clattered. Even though she couldn't see it from where she was, he angled the screen.

Ánte: *My mom doesn't think I should hang out with you.*

Erik sent a thinking emoji that had a hand on its chin.

Erik: *What could she possibly be thinking about me?*

Ánte: *Probably that you're going to kidnap me.*

Erik: *But seriously?*

Ánte: *She thinks that you're, well, a bad influence on me but I don't get it.*

Erik replied with two yellow figures laughing so hard they cried. Ánte glanced at his mother. Why did she get to decide who he should and shouldn't hang out with?

Erik: *But wait.*

Erik: *Isn't your birthday in July? You're older than me.*

Ánte snorted. It was nothing more than a noisy breath through his nose, but his mother turned and looked at him. He didn't reply until she returned to what she'd been doing.

Ánte: *Maybe I'm the one who's a bad influence on you.*

Erik: *Yeah, probably.*

He didn't know what else to write. Took a bite from his sandwich, let the cheese melt in his mouth. Erik was quiet too, but then the dots appeared next to the picture again. Ánte swallowed.

Erik: *My parents are going to a party tonight.*

Ánte: *Good for them.*

Erik: *And for me.*

Erik: *Thought I'd invite you and Máhttu and Juhán over. We could game or something. Coming?*

Ánte: *Did you forget that I'm not supposed to hang out with you?*

Erik: *You're not hanging out with just me.*

Erik: *So I can't kidnap you.*

Erik sent a big, blue hand doing a thumbs-up. Ánte put his phone down and stared out in the kitchen. At his mom's back by the sink, the empty chairs by the table.

A million little birds filled his stomach, their feathers tickling the stomach lining. He took a mouthful of juice. Filled his glass again. Drank. Just to have something to do. His mom would probably be able to tell if he planned to go to Erik's. Did he have it in him to discuss it? If Máhttu and Juhán would be there too, it might not even be worth it.

It was still morning, many hours left until evening. He checked the time anyway, as if it would change anything. The sun made its way through the kitchen window, blinded him.

“Ánte.” His mom put the dish brush down and looked at him. “I want to apologize for yesterday. It was uncalled for, sounding that harsh.”

The apology just made him more irritated.

“Uh-huh.”

“Won’t you at least look at me?”

He met her eyes without putting his phone down. When it dinged he couldn’t resist reading it. His mother sighed.

Erik: *What do you say?*

Ánte: *Guess I’ll be there.*

HE FLINCHED WHEN he heard the knock on the front door. What if it was Erik? But why would it be? Whoever was out there, the person would have seen him moving through the entryway window.

"Can you get the door?" his mother called from the living room.

He opened it. On the porch stood Lasse, peering into the entryway.

"Hi, Ánte," he said. "Got any coffee in this house?"

"Yes," Ánte said, stepping back into the house. He shoved his hand in his pocket, found a loose thread, pulled. Looked down at Lasse's shoes. They ended up on the entryway rug when Lasse stepped out of them.

"I head back to Stockholm tomorrow already," Lasse said. "I've barely had a chance to visit with you all."

Ánte looked at the clock on the wall above the dresser. Twelve. Unbelievable that the hand of a clock could move that slowly. You could stare at it forever and it still wouldn't move a millimeter.

His mom joined them in the entryway, so quietly you hardly noticed.

"Nice of you to stop by." She smiled at Lasse. "I'll get the coffee started."

Ánte's dad was sitting at the kitchen table when Lasse walked in. Ánte stayed back in the entryway, heard *Hello there,* and *Wow, time flies.*

"Come and have some fika," his mom called.

Ánte walked slowly into the kitchen, sank down in the same chair as that morning.

"How are things down there in Gay City?" his dad asked, chuckling. He picked up a cinnamon roll from the plate and leaned back. "You have any snow in the winter?"

"Not much," Lasse replied. "But otherwise, it's okay."

"And the women? Still the same wife?"

"I've been married for ten years, actually."

"That's fucking crazy," his dad said. You could see the roll in his mouth when he spoke. "And the quality of the dames down there? They know how to make palt?"

Ánte's mom put a cup out for his dad and one for Lasse, poured coffee. She left the pot on the table. The copper surface shone.

She put a glass bottle with yellow soda, an orange on the paper label, in front of Ánte.

Ánte looked at her, his forehead creased. "You didn't think I might want coffee?"

She shook her head and smiled, handed him a bottle opener as she sat down. He opened the bottle with a click. The soda fizzed on his tongue.

"The dames in Stockholm can definitely cook all kinds of things," Lasse said, looking at the soda bottle. He took a mouthful of coffee. "But, you see, I'm married to a man."

His dad laughed. Then he got quiet.

"Though Ruben actually makes great shredded reindeer," Lasse continued. "Sunná usually tries to get us some meat after the slaughter."

Ánte looked down at the table. Traced the plaid pattern on the table mat with his nail. Wasn't anybody going to say something? The silence was unbearable.

He looked up, caught Lasse's eye. Lasse lifted his cup to his mouth. The brown paint on the edge of the cup had worn off. When he leaned his head back and drank, he winked. Quickly, then he looked away, looked at something else, something that wasn't Ánte.

"Ruben?" his dad said finally. He scratched his beard. "From town?"

Lasse nodded.

"We moved down there together. But we do feel a little homesick."

"I'm not surprised," his dad said. His laughter sounded a little like barking. "Damn, but I don't think I would have made it through a single winter without my Lynx."

Ánte swallowed and swallowed. Tried to not look at his dad too much but couldn't help it. His dad's face had taken on a reddish tone, as if he had a sunburn.

"It would have been good for you actually," his mom said.

She turned from his dad to Lasse. Ánte might be imagining it, but he thought she looked relieved.

"Is Ruben here now?"

Lasse shook his head.

"How is he?"

"Better."

"The two of you will have to come up together sometime," she said. "We've not seen him for a long time."

"We'll do that."

That was when Ánte realized that he had been holding his breath. He inhaled. His lungs expanded. This was not breathing; it was something bigger.

Lasse started telling them about the house they had bought, discussed heating pumps with his dad. But Ánte no longer heard them, could no longer focus. He saw their facial expressions but couldn't make out any words.

Then Lasse stood up.

"Thank you so much for the coffee, Ánne-Máret. I have to get going."

His mom and dad stood up too, wished Lasse good luck on his trip, asked him to say hi to Ruben and come back soon. Ánte stayed seated. Looked around the room. The wallpaper blurred and the furniture was softening around the edges.

Lasse put his hand on his shoulder and squeezed.

"Let's keep in touch, buddy."

ÁNTE RAN, HIS FEET pounded down the porch, his heart pounded even faster. The soles of his shoes hit the asphalt. When his parents asked him where he was going, he'd told them he had something to say to Lasse. Something he'd forgotten to tell him.

Lasse had walked pretty far. Ánte called after him, moved faster when he got no response. Then, finally, Lasse seemed to hear him. He turned around and Ánte stopped. The wind grabbed his back, pushed him forward another step.

"I've already experienced it."

"Excuse me?"

"You said love is like a drug, but it's exactly the opposite. It's like medicine."

A tiny smile made the wrinkles by Lasse's eyes spread across his face. Behind him, along the side of the road, the trees were turning green.

"I want you to promise me something then."

"What?"

The leaves of the sprouting birch trees sparkled. High, high up in the sky danced the crowns of the pines.

There was a playful twinkle in Lasse's eyes.

"Promise me to be braver than I was."

"WE'RE OFF," ERIK'S MOTHER said, winding a scarf around her neck. She gave Erik a stern look. "No alcohol, no drugs, no girls."

"Yeah, yeah," he said. "Goodbye."

She stroked his cheek before she left. He glanced at Ánte, made a face.

The gravel made a crunching sound when the car backed out of the yard. As soon as it had disappeared along the road, Erik locked the door. The birds in Ánte's stomach woke up.

"Juhán and Máhttu aren't even writing back." Erik took his phone out. "They must have spaced or something."

"Aha."

Erik's fingers moved across the screen. He always looked so focused when he wrote. Almost irritated. When he was done, his face lit up in a smile.

"What do you want to do while we wait?"

Ánte shrugged.

"They'll probably get back to me soon," Erik said.

He walked to his room, sat down on his bed and leaned against a pillow. Ánte sat too, stiffly, carefully. Didn't know how to act.

Erik had reindeer antlers on his wall. On the tines hung handcrafted knives, guvse, a black cap with a Fiskflyg logo. A meter or so from the antler a large television had been mounted. Ánte looked at Erik's hand on the bedspread. His fingers looked soft. The thumbnail was a tiny bit shorter than the rest of his nails.

"What are you looking at?" Erik asked.

Ánte jumped.

"Um, nothing."

They sat in silence. Ánte's stomach was a roller coaster. His thoughts refused to be quiet. What if Juhán and Máhttu didn't show up? Then what would they do? Though Ánte wanted to be alone with Erik, that thought was almost unbearable now.

Erik was staring at his phone, a tiny wrinkle on his forehead.

"I think my mom bought popcorn," he said finally.

Ánte's eyes caressed Erik's back when he stood up. He made a fist so hard it hurt.

Erik found the popcorn on the top shelf of the pantry, threw the bag in the microwave and leaned against the sink. His T-shirt had slid up his belly a little, a sliver of skin showing above the edge of his pants.

The popcorn thrummed wildly in the bag. Erik looked at his phone, Ánte just stood there. Looked at the plants on the windowsill. Didn't know what to do with his hands. Where did you usually keep them when standing up? He tried putting them in his pockets. Let them hang by his side. Nothing felt right.

The microwave dinged and Erik put his phone on the bench. The smell of burnt butter seeped from the bag when he opened it.

The screen on Erik's phone lit up. Ánte barely had time to glimpse her name, but he did. His heart cramped with anxiety, squeezed.

"Are you texting with Julia?"

Erik poured the popcorn into a bowl, picked out the most burnt ones. Something in his face had changed.

"Why?"

Why? Hadn't they broken up? What else had Erik meant when he said they had talked?

Ánte shrugged. Tried to ignore the feelings that came rushing in.

"Just wondering."

Erik held the bowl out but Ánte shook his head. Neither of them took any popcorn. Erik put his phone in his pocket, wiped something from his eye.

"I don't understand her anymore," he said.

Ánte didn't want to hear Erik talk about Julia anymore. At first, it had made him feel hopeful, but now it just felt confusing.

"You don't?"

"Not that she understands me either."

Everything inside Ánte felt so dark that he had to do something about it. Find a way to rid himself of this heavy feeling.

"Maybe . . . ," he said. "Julia was kidnapped by an alien, and that's who's posting on Messenger."

"Um, what?"

"Get it? The alien tries to write like Julia, so you won't know that she's been kidnapped. But that's the kind of thing people notice."

"You're a weirdo."

"Well, think about it," Ánte said. It worked; laughter bubbled out from behind his words. Swept over the darkness. "You have to agree it's a little funny."

"What the hell." Erik laughed, his body shaking. "Did you take something before you got here?"

Ánte used his hands to show how big the alien's head had been. Erik's face cracked up. He shoved Ánte below his collarbone. Ánte's stomach muscles ached. He took a handful of popcorn from the bowl and threw it at Erik. Erik shook his head, took a step closer and Ánte was caught.

They ended up close, centimeters from each other. The sink pushed against Ánte's lower back. The laughter was gone. Ánte counted his heartbeats, wondered how many he would have left after this. Far from enough, probably.

They stood so close that he could smell Erik. There was a note of something sweet, something soft, something purely Erik. Time passed, second by second. Erik didn't move. Ánte didn't either.

Everything was now.

Now, now, *now*.

Carefully, he touched Erik, as if he might break. A bird heart in his hand. He moved one finger over his cheek, throat, neck. Erik stood still, quiet.

Their eyes met. Ánte almost fell, but there it was, under his feet, the floor. He managed to stay upright. Must not lose it now when it was so close. Erik was so incredibly close. But not close enough.

"Ánte," Erik said. A tiny shard of disbelief.

Ánte's muscles tensed, his breathing stopped. His whole body waited—he had never done anything but wait for this.

Erik pulled back a few centimeters, but it felt like kilometers. His eyes roamed, searched Ánte's face. Paused at his lips. Much too long.

Erik's mouth grazed his. His lips were as light as feathers, a bandage on a body bleeding to death. Ánte put his hand on Erik's neck, pulled him closer.

His skeleton caught fire.

Ánte's fingers trembled against Erik's skin. He let them wander through his hair, felt the short neck hairs under his nails, standing straight up, tickling his fingertips.

Erik's lips were soft, careful, then hard. A tiny sound from his mouth. His body was warm, the T-shirt bunched up between them. Ánte probed the edge of the material, hot skin beneath it.

He followed the waistband of Erik's pants with his finger. Couldn't breathe when Erik's mouth was so close. All the breaths he had taken until this moment would have to be enough.

A vibration against his leg. Something hard and warm pushed against his body and his blood began to flow faster. His body was jerking, emotions in charge now. All he wanted was to get closer. Wanted to be on top of Erik, beneath him, inside him.

A second later: Erik's tight fist on his chest. Pushing him away. Cold air rushed in between their bodies, rushed into Ánte's lungs. Erik backed off and pulled his phone from his pocket. It vibrated a few more times.

"Julia," he said.

Ánte sank down on the floor, his back against the kitchen cabinets.

His lips were sore, still warm, like open wounds in his face. His pulse thundered; he had been running but come to a sudden stop. He looked down in his lap, pulled his knees to his stomach. Closed his eyes. Ordered his body to obey, but it refused to listen.

He wished he could understand what was going on in Erik's head, but he couldn't.

Why did Erik care about Julia now? *Now,* of all times?

Erik sat down on a kitchen chair. Ánte looked at his feet. His mind wanted to escape, go somewhere else.

As Erik read, he held the phone close to his eyes. Something was breaking in his face. His lips were trembling. Ánte had never seen him like this. There was a sharp pain in his heart.

Erik slammed the phone down on the table.

"What the hell am I doing?"

Ánte was wondering the same thing. He looked down at his own hands. They were still shaking. Hands that had touched Erik, that had been so close to his skin. He would never let them touch anything else.

Erik's steps creaked across the floor. He hunched down in front of Ánte, who looked straight into his broken eyes. The color had cracked in there. A dark iris broken in two.

"Say something," Erik said.

"You're the one who should say something this time."

Erik stood up, turned away from Ánte. Shook his head over and over. The popcorn had turned cold on the counter. Erik whacked the bowl so it flew off the counter and landed on the wooden floorboards with a clatter. One tiny popcorn kernel ended up in the crease of Ánte's arm. It had a black edge.

Ánte stood. His knees protested, but his legs carried him. He touched Erik's shoulder lightly. Wanted to hold him, tight, tight, but Erik shrugged his hand off. Didn't turn around. Ánte took one reluctant step away from him. Then another.

Tiny white clouds crunched under his feet when he left.

MURMURING VOICES REACHED Ánte from the living room as he entered the house. He snuck in quietly. The evening light seeped inside and lit up the house, a sliver of sun across the cool floor. He threw his socks in the laundry basket. Walked barefoot into his room and closed the door.

The ceiling stared vacantly at him when he lay down on his bed. White. Emotionless. He wished the entire room had been white. Maybe he could paint it. Take out every piece of furniture, every item, every feeling, every memory. There was nothing that didn't remind him of Erik.

He felt empty. Numb. His body had shut down. It felt as if nothing had happened.

As if years had gone by since he kissed Erik.

He picked up his phone and went to Erik's Facebook profile page. Locked his phone, unlocked it again. Didn't want to see Erik ever again but wanted only to see him.

He scrolled down the page and read every single post, from the bottom up. Game reviews, music suggestions, strange conversations from four years ago. Erik had been married when he was thirteen. Everybody wondered who the lucky lady was. Softie Handson, Juhán had suggested. Erik had replied with an emoji with its tongue out.

The higher up Ánte got in the thread, the fewer the posts. He was getting closer to the post that always made his stomach turn. Knew he was almost there. This time he actually wanted to see it.

There it was.

In a relationship with Julia Stenman.

He looked at the pictures of Erik and Julia, next to each other but not together. Above: a tiny blue heart. The comments were full of congratulations. He read every single word until he knew them by heart. *Mother-in-law's dream,* one woman with the same last name as Julia had written. Julia had replied with five hearts.

It still didn't hurt.

He clicked his way into Julia's profile and looked at her pictures. Zoomed in on her lips, shaped into a kissy mouth. Lips that had touched Erik a hundred times. And yet, the feeling that filled his body was not dark, not painful. His lips had touched Erik's too.

He closed the Facebook page and opened Instagram. The pictures from the half anniversary were gone from Erik's account. He quickly went to Julia's account. Not a single picture of Erik—only selfies and cat pictures. Not a trace left of him.

Ánte put his phone down. Even though the shades were drawn in his room, the sun had still managed to make its way inside, paint wavy stripes on his hands. It had found a spot in the sky that it liked—Ánte knew that soon, it would not move for a very long time. It would stay all summer.

Soon, nothing would be able to keep the light out.

HIS MOTHER'S HAND in his hair. She stroked it in the wrong direction. Hugged him from behind, sniffed his neck.

"Can you help me with the groceries?"

Any other time, he would have escaped her grip, muttered, sighed, but something was different now. He let her hold him. Needed the warmth and the closeness for a little while.

"Okay."

Four full bags stood on the kitchen counter. One of them had ripped a little at the edge. His mom always shopped for a whole week. She put grapes in the refrigerator, a bunch of bananas in the fruit bowl on the table. Ánte piled yogurt containers on top of one another.

"Hey," his mom said, "I want to ask you something."

"Yes?"

It took a while before she continued.

"Were you at Erik's last night?"

"Probably not. I didn't exactly forget you chewing me out in the car."

She shook her head.

"But you did go somewhere."

"Yes, with Máhttu and Juhán."

"Why wasn't Erik with you?"

A milk carton slipped from his hand and landed on the floor with a thud.

"Are you serious?"

His mom sighed. She picked up the milk and put it in the refrigerator.

"I've apologized," she said. "But I'm not the only one who's been unfair."

Ánte picked up a blood orange, started peeling the sticker off with his nail.

"It seems to be okay for some people."

"What?"

"You know what I mean."

The refrigerator had been open so long that it started beeping. His mom closed it, started putting groceries in the pantry instead.

"What I'm really trying to tell you is that your dad and I have talked."

"Okay?" The fruit was warm in his hand.

Her eyes on the shelves, she said:

"We just want you to be happy."

Ánte noticed that he had scratched a hole in the orange peel. He put the fruit down on the kitchen counter. His hand shook.

"What do you mean?"

"I mean that how you choose to live your life is up to you. We're here for you, no matter what." His mother closed the pantry, turned to Ánte, touched his shoulder gently. "I don't think I have to understand everything. I can still love you." She pulled him toward her. "And I do. I love you so much it hurts. We both do."

Ánte let his chin rest on his mom's shoulder. Looked at the sun rays on the kitchen counter. The blood oranges.

Her voice close to his ear.

"Nothing in the whole world can change that."

ÁNTE FELT ERIK'S FOOTSTEPS even before Erik came into the room. Felt the rattling in his rib cage. How the wooden floor planks gave way.

Erik's frame appeared in the doorway. His hair was darker than usual, a drop of water had landed on his shoulder. He startled when he saw Ánte sitting on his bed. A crease between his eyebrows. Ánte counted the seconds. One, two, three. Seven, before Erik's lips moved.

"What are you doing here?"

"Your mom said I could wait here while you took a shower. So, I just, well, waited."

"Okay."

Erik was gripping the door frame. Ánte wanted to touch his knuckles. Put his fingertips in the depressions between them.

He lifted his hand, then let it sink back into his lap. Lifted it again, raked it through his hair. No little birds were fluttering in his stomach anymore—they were eagles.

"You're doing that thing again," Erik said.

"What?"

"With your hair."

Before Erik appeared, he had known what he was going to say, but now his words were caught behind walls of rock. For every second that went by a new one was built.

He stayed quiet.

Erik let go of the door frame. He pushed his newly washed bangs from his face and closed the door. His scent reached Ánte from where he stood. Ánte inhaled through his nose as if this were the last oxygen in the world.

The mattress sank when Erik sat down on the bed. Ánte's words sank too. Far, far down in his body. Erik leaned forward, braided his fingers over his knees.

"Why are you here?"

Ánte dug around among words and sentences, remembered what he had promised Lasse.

"I was thinking," he said, "about what happened."

"But you had nothing to say."

"Neither did you."

Erik turned and Ánte swallowed his exhale. He focused on the tiny movement in the corner of Erik's mouth. It felt like his entire life depended on it.

"I just don't know how to do this."

He wasn't sure what Erik meant but he nodded. Something was opening up inside his chest. Something large.

"Try," Ánte said. Try whatever you want.

"What?"

Ánte's mouth was open, his words on his tongue, just lying there, trembling, not knowing if they would dare fall. Should they?

Erik rubbed his hands over his thighs.

"I texted with Julia after you left."

The sentence that had been building inside Ánte's lips fell apart. He shook his head a little. Didn't know if he wanted to hear anymore.

"She asked if I had made up my mind," Erik continued.

Ánte swallowed. Looked at Erik, who was looking at the floor, eyelashes fluttering, something shiny behind them.

"What did you tell her?"

Erik took a deep breath.

"Yes."

Three hard knocks on the door. Helene opened before they could answer. Ánte stiffened, didn't know where to put his hands. Fumbled with them in his lap.

"What?" Erik said.

Helene smiled at Ánte. In response, he pulled up the corners of his mouth. Didn't know if it looked like a real smile. His lips didn't work like they should.

"Just thought I'd see if you wanted something," she said. "There's still some of the cake I made left."

She looked at them quizzically. Erik shrugged.

"You can go get a couple of slices," she said.

She pulled the door closed but not all the way. It started opening again with a little squeak.

"Parents can't close doors," Erik said. "Have you noticed?"

"I've noticed."

Ánte looked at the strand of hair that had escaped down Erik's forehead. At his birthmarks, three tiny stars. What had Erik decided?

The corners of Erik's mouth were pulled up. Ánte looked at him, searchingly.

"What?"

Erik shook his head. Grinned. Ánte wanted to reach over and touch every millimeter of his face with his lips.

Oh god.

He glanced at the gap in the doorway. Could almost hear Helene breathing outside. He couldn't go on like this. If Erik didn't say something soon, there was nothing else that Ánte could do. He could hardly breathe.

Erik's eyes, Erik's eyes, Erik's eyes.

Ánte stood up and brushed something invisible from his jeans.

"I think I have to go," he said.

Erik stood up too but didn't say anything. Ánte shifted his weight onto one foot. Changed feet. The eagles flapped, their wings touching his stomach lining. The feathers reached all the way up his throat.

"I guess I'll see you later."

Erik nodded, eyes stuck on Ánte's. Ánte couldn't stand still. If he raised his arms, his feet would lift off the floor.

He managed to stay put. To stay still.

"I'll leave then." He looked at Erik's lips, waited for them to move. But they didn't. "See you."

One, two steps toward the door.

"Ánte."

His heart was not moving when he turned around. Erik came closer, shoved his foot against the door. It closed with a click. He lifted his hand and touched Ánte's fingers, waited.

Erik's lips were very close to Ánte's.

"Stay," he said.

ÁNTE BURIED HIS LIPS in the depression by Erik's collarbone. Kissed him along his neck, toward his ear. Gently nibbled his earlobe, allowing his teeth to touch skin. Put his nose in Erik's armpit. It was as if all of Erik's smells had gotten lodged there.

He put his ear to Erik's chest and listened, the heart beating in a safe, even rhythm. He felt Erik's breath on his scalp, heating his whole body. He wanted to go through his entire life dressed in Erik's breath. Not listen to anything but the sound of his heart.

Erik's skin was hot, burning against his ear. When had it gotten so warm? They were both soaked in sweat. Ánte pulled himself up to a sitting position and opened the window a little. A warm breeze made the curtain flap.

Then he saw them, the flames. Clouds bursting in red, pink, orange. A flaming fire from the sky. A fire burning the entire world—the room, the bed, their bodies, their very bones.

But it was not the end of the world. He understood this now. It was the opposite.

HE OPENED HIS WEB BROWSER. The words appeared when he clicked on the search field; his phone already knew. The search showed the same results it always had, the results he had already scrolled through.

The Flashback headings were purple from being clicked on before. A bruise that changed colors.

For the first time, he created an account on the forum. Made up a meaningless username, a name that nobody would remember. It didn't matter—he never wanted to log on again.

The words flew like bullets through the screen as he scrolled down. He ducked at every single one. Clicked Reply.

We exist, he wrote. *And we're alive.*

AUTHOR'S NOTE

This is a fictitious story. Parts of it are based on real events that in some cases have been adapted to fit the story.

The racial biology mentioned in this book is a real part of Sweden's history. The character Harald Lundgren is partially based on Herman Lundborg, the director for the State Institute for Racial Biology in Uppsala in the early 1900s. According to racial biologists, humans were made up of different "races" who were deemed to be of different worth. They wanted to prevent the "Swedish race" from mixing with races they saw as inferior. The Sámi people were seen as belonging to a lower-standing race.

Lundborg's research has been criticized for not having produced results of any significance.

THE LANTERN PAPERBACKS DESIGN

The design of Lantern Paperbacks was originated by Filip Peraić. He says: "The Lantern Paperbacks needed a visual identity which symbolizes their beautiful mission of 'spreading light into the world.' This brief was brought to life through a colorful line look, led by our special 'L' mark, formed by nine rays of light."